A. (Auguste) Gratry

Henri Perreyve

A. (Auguste) Gratry

Henri Perreyve

ISBN/EAN: 9783744660037

Printed in Europe, USA, Canada, Australia, Japan

Cover: Foto ©Raphael Reischuk / pixelio.de

More available books at **www.hansebooks.com**

HENRI PERREYVE

RIVINGTONS

London	Waterloo Place
Oxford	High Street
Cambridge	Trinity Street

By A. GRATRY

Prêtre de l'Oratoire, Professeur de Morale Évangélique à la
Sorbonne, et Membre de l'Académie Française

Translated by Special Permission

By the Author of

"A Dominican Artist," "Life of S. Francis de Sales,"

etc., etc.

RIVINGTONS

London, Oxford, and Cambridge

1872

CONTENTS.

INTRODUCTION.

THE original intention of this book was to offer
to English readers a sketch of the singularly
gifted author of the "Journée des Malades;" a work
which has rarely failed to become as a living presence,
a loved friend, to those who have once taken it up,
more especially if they have done so in sickness,
weariness, and suffering. It seemed probable that those
who prized the book would care to know how intensely
real it is, how Henri Perreyve in the first freshness of
youth and of a rare intellect had proved every trial of
which he wrote. He had tested the trial of returning
day, which brings life and vigour interest and hope to
the strong, but weary, helpless hours of depression to
the sick man, set aside from the work he once delighted
to perform. He knew the need of a friendly voice to
whisper that there is still work for such as these to
do:—"l'ouvrage des hommes sur la terre ne se mesure
pas à la quantité de leurs forces physiques, mais à la
qualité de leur volonté." He knew how to accept
sacrifice as the highest work, and how, too, no work
can be worthy to be offered to God unless the spirit

of sacrifice be in it. He knew the trial and the blessing of solitude—"alone with God;" he knew how suffering is an inevitable part of the training of those who are to carry God's choicest gifts of consolation to their brethren. "Celui qui n'a pas souffert, aurait-il le cœur le plus tendre et l'esprit le plus pénétrant, ne peut rien connaitre à la souffrance des hommes. Il en parle comme l'aveugle disserte des couleurs. . . L'expérience seule du mal peut briser cette glace, et donner le don de consolation." Henri Perreyve has seemed like an intimate friend to many whose earthly path he never crossed; probably because what he says of Rosa Ferrucci was so singularly true of himself, "Il y a des âmes qui trouvent Dieu partout."

Probably no heart which has been brought face to face with death,—which has watched those dearer far than aught save God pass within that "transfiguration;" which has pondered upon the inevitable hour as nearing itself—but would listen with deep interest to the Abbé Eugène Bernard's exquisitely touching record of his more than brother's deathbed. There is a fascination to most of us in knowing how others have met that which is so surely, so rapidly, advancing upon each one of us; a stay in realizing with what special individual loving care the dear Master Who Himself vouchsafed to die for His children leads every human soul through the cold shadow. It may be as Henri Perreyve says, that "à travers les différences des âges, des conditions, des génies, toutes les saintes morts se ressemblent; c'est toujours l'amour dirigeant la mort et la transfigurant en sacrifice." But we crave to hear how love dealt with death in each case anew—we would fain catch one ray of the transfiguration to cheer our hearts under the sacrifice. And surely no one can live over those "last days" with him without feeling better able to look over to the other side of Jordan, more confident in His Aid Who will not fail to be there.

The first intention, then, of this little book, was to gather together, by the kind consent of the R. Père Gratry and others, all that would best serve to bring their beloved Henri before us; but his life, though remarkable in its vigour of purpose, intellectual brilliancy, and intensity of self-devotion, was uneventful as far as outer circumstance is concerned. "The great act, almost the only event of his life," as the Père Gratry says, "was his choice of a vocation." But while there is little to record of historical facts concerning his life, the great philosopher and metaphysician has lifted a veil from the hidden workings of Henri Perreyve's heart, and has given us an insight into a world of thought not often so freely opened to sight. He has laid before us a page of the inner life of

a gifted young man, influenced as men will be perhaps
the more in proportion to their gifts, by the influences
of the strangely wild, exciting, rapid times in which
we live. And at this moment especially, when such
mighty and rugged questions are struggling in the
hearts of all thinking people, when to reconcile progress, liberty, equality, and the like ideas with the
highest, purest spiritual truth and life is so sore a per-
plexity to many, it has been thought that the opinions
of one so eminent in the Church, and be it said with
all loving respect, in the cause of progress and liberty,
will be read with a special interest.

"Signa autem temporum non potestis scire?" the
Père Gratry asks. And he does not shrink from
affirming boldly that the Great First Cause of all tem-
porary movement is God: the movement no doubt
perverted and distorted in endless ways by man, but
nevertheless to be met and set forward and guided.
"It is the perversion, not the movement, we must
strive to check," the Abbé exclaims. His thoughts
concerning many topics of the day, full of the deepest
interest to us all; education, vocation, the priesthood,
organization of the priest's life, its ministry, its
hindrances—have taken shape as he wrote concerning
his dearly loved disciple and friend; and it is believed that there are many kindred minds among
ourselves who will welcome a closer and more

familiar approach to the thoughts and opinions of one so deservedly esteemed and venerated by the whole Church. And therefore the sketch called "Henri Perreyve" has not been tampered with, but is offered to English readers in its original form, *i.e.* rather a series of essays than a biography; completed, as indeed it could not otherwise be, by the brief records called " Derniers Jours de l'Abbé Henri Perreyve " by M. l'Abbé Bernard.

I believe many people habitually begin a book in the middle ; I would suggest to those who read this book *not* to "begin at the beginning," but to read Henri Perreyve's forcible letters, Père Gratry's fervent words on the priestly office, and the Abbé Bernard's most touching record of Henri's last days, first, and then to turn to the Père Gratry's remarks upon education, vocation, &c., under the light cast upon them by those passages.

Henri Perreyve will probably be better known both in France and England as the author of the " Journée des Malades" than through any of his other writings. But the same peculiarity of style, the exceeding purity and clearness, the thorough reality, which give a charm to that book, are to be found in his other writings ; and those who will read more especially his biographical essays on Lacordaire, Rosa

Ferrucci, his friends Hermann de Jouffroy, Alfred
Tonnellé, and his beloved teacher Mgr. Baudry, as
also his "Station à la Sorbonne"—the last sermons
preached by him—cannot fail to find the greatest
charm both in style and substance. Nor must it be
forgotten that we owe that matchless volume of
Lacordaire's familiar intercourse with the younger
generation he loved so well "Lettres à des Jeunes
Gens" to the Abbé Perreyve, to whom many of those
exquisitely beautiful letters were addressed. During
the last weeks of his life Henri Perreyve sketched
the plan of a work specially intended for young men
on Religious and Social Life, which would doubtless
have been a great boon to all ages, had it been God's
Will that the undertaking should have gone farther.

How fervently he believed that the service wrought
for God and His people is not arrested not suspen-
ded by death, only transferred elsewhere, only raised
to a truer higher more lasting sphere where the
chill of disappointment and the check of error can
never come, we find on all sides.

"I am not very far on in life," he wrote, speaking
of his friend Alfred Tonnellé's death, "yet I have
been called to speak of several who have passed away,
all young and bright, all cut off, as men say, prematurely, and torn from what seemed such useful lives,
so precious to God's work. But what is life indeed,

what are all the deeds of man, the pride of earthly hopes? What is the world's estimate of minds, or the structure it thinks to build on this or the other human career? What is there really true, really worth seeking save a simple faith which gives itself up to the guidance of a Heavenly Master, striving day by day bravely to fulfil a task which His Glory does not really need, and to fall asleep at night with those words on our lips which can only be justly said by such as have worked well—'Lord, we are unprofitable servants'?"

Non nobis, Domine, non nobis, sed Nomini Tuo da
Gloriam.

Those who have the nearest and dearest right to cherish Henri Perreyve's memory are preparing for publication a collection of his letters, which can hardly fail to be a most welcome gift to the Church. Together with this mention let there be combined an expression of most hearty affectionate thanks to those, bound to him both by natural and spiritual ties, who have so cordially forwarded this attempt to make him loved and known in England as well as in France.

Epiphany, 1872.

While these last lines were actually in the press, one of those alluded to has passed beyond the veil —the " bon et cher Père," to whom Henri Perreyve owed so much ; the learned eloquent member of the Académie Française, so esteemed and revered among men, the humble-minded holy priest whose inner life in all its saintliness is known to none save the Angels and their Lord—the Père Gratry.

The venerable Abbé Gratry entered upon his rest on Feb. 6th, 1872, at Montreux, on the Lake of Geneva, after much severe suffering. Surely we may quote his own words spoken of his much loved spiritual child, Henri Perreyve :—" Ce jour là vous étiez porté par les anges. Je crois à ces gracieux détails de providence : *In manibus portabunt te, ne forte offendas ad lapidem pedem tuum.* Les anges vous ont porté pendant toute votre vie, et jusque dans le sein de Dieu." What can better express the feeling of those who love him than the tender words spoken by Henri Perreyve concerning one they both loved, Hermann de Jouffroy?—" Quand on meurt, après une telle vie, dans la grace qui fait les saints, et les lèvres collées sur la Croix du Sauveur, on passe, des demeures terrestres, dans le cœur même de Dieu.

Aussi, je vous l'avoue, dès le premier instant de calme qui suivit les surprises de la douleur, je ne pus voir notre ami que transfiguré dans cet amour éternel qu'on appelle le ciel. Comment le plaindre ? comment nous plaindre ? Il voit, il sait maintenant ! Cette intelligence ardente, cette volonté courageuse, ce cœur généreux et profond, sont couronnés et rassasiés. Il possède dans leur foyer les rayons divins dont il poursuivait laborieusement ici-bas les traces fugitives !"

We cannot but call to mind how Père Gratry delighted to dwell upon Henri Perreyve's parting words to a dearly loved friend, " Nous ne cesserons point, n'est ce pas, de travailler ensemble à la cause de Dieu et de son Eglise ?" or his fervent belief in "the friendly group of real living souls awaiting each one of us on the other shore of the narrow stream of death ;" for while to us who are left death is a darkening and a disappearance of those we love, to those who are gone before we may humbly believe that it is a bright joyous dawning. And as his fervent prayer was " Oh, Saviour, teach us to live, teach us to die. Give us grace ever to remember Thy promise ' Whosoever liveth and believeth in Me shall never die '," who can doubt it has been answered, and the mighty lesson of life and death has been learned ? "To none is death so little of a change, as to those

whose life has been one long unbroken confidence in
God."

O ye Holy and Humble Men of Heart, bless ye the
  Lord, Praise Him and Magnify Him for Ever.

Quinquagesima, 1872.

HENRI PERREYVE

CHAPTER I.

HENRI PERREYVE—EDUCATION.

I SHOULD not have accepted the trust committed to me by the Faculté de Théologie of pronouncing the *Éloge* of our beloved colleague and friend (I had well nigh said our child) Henri Perreyve —I should have preferred to commune silently with my grief for his loss, had I not felt that in this case it is no mere question of panegyric, but of a most holy lesson to be read ; and that the trust devolving upon me is to set forth the example of his singularly beautiful life to that rising generation whom he loved, and who loved him so well. Taken from us so prematurely, it remains for me to gather up the threads of his brief life, and, to borrow a Scriptural expression, " raise up seed to our brother." Who can doubt that his labours, his writings, his life, his sufferings, and death, will be blessed by their influence in moulding other men to his likeness ! Nor can I refrain here from expressing the deep conviction of my own soul, that in Henri Perreyve we look upon a most rare example of perfect manly beauty.   All who knew him agree on this point, that the one characteristic which stamps his outward life and his inward soul is only to be expressed by that word BEAUTY. All the inward beauty wherewith courage, intelligence, devotion, and goodness can invest a soul ; and all the outward expression of beauty with which such a soul can stamp the living man were combined in him : Nature and Grace had alike done their very best for him ; he overflowed with their choicest gifts.

What love he won from all ! Perhaps he was the man whom Père Lacordaire loved best of all the world ; it was to Henri that that noble soul addressed the words, "You live eternally in my heart, as my son and my friend." His exquisite moral beauty was the means of raising, guiding, comforting many a soul ; worthy follower therein of his Master, Whose it is to "ride on prosperously because of truth, and meekness, and righteousness." "*Specie tua et pulchritudine tua intende, prospere procede, et regna.*"[1] His whole life was but one noble, earnest effort to follow his Master's Call ; that call which sets no lower ideal of life before the Christian than one of absolute moral beauty, the very Beauty of God Himself. " Be ye perfect even as your Father Which is

[1] Ps. xlv. 4.

in Heaven is Perfect." There is but one way to attain this height, either practically or intellectually; and that is, to aim ceaselessly at all that is highest, noblest, most beautiful; and of all the men I have ever known, this dear brother pursued such an aim most earnestly.

One cannot but pause to ask, whither did these ceaseless efforts to attain the summit of moral beauty lead him? To the Priesthood—that is, to the highest aim of life; to that sacred dignity of which he himself speaks as " the joy of joys—the sole object of my whole existence!"[1] And so, as I trace the outlines of his beauty, I find myself practically dwelling upon the dignity of the Sacerdotal office, and exhorting other men to do the like. Nor would I limit such exhortation to a single class. For while I speak chiefly of the highest of all Sacerdotal offices, the ministry of the Gospel in the Eternal Church, my words are also applicable to a much wider reach of thought. Is there not a priesthood of education, a priesthood of science, a priesthood of art, of self-devotion and charity, not to omit that most true priesthood of the father at the head of his family? Every duty fulfilled to God, every good deed, every light reflected from God, and shed by man upon his

[1] "Cette joie des joies, et cette unique raison de toute ma vie!"

fellow-man, is a Sacerdotal act ; and therefore I repeat
it, my exhortation is addressed to every Christian, or,
what is practically the same, to every one who, as in
God's Sight, possesses a true loving heart. But above
all, to our young men, Henri Perreyve's life, his letters,
and his writings speak forth in the most earnest of all
possible exhortations to priestly self-devotion. Let us
kindle our dull hearts by contemplating this gracious
model of true moral beauty.

I.

The history of his outer life is brief. Henri Perreyve was born April 11th, 1831, at Paris. His
parents are living yet, and the sister who was as a
second mother to him. We may not speak of them,
save to count them thrice blessed of God in their
son,—that son whom He has taken from them for a
while.

Henri's[1] first real studies were in art and religion.
He attended college lectures with no special interest;
although by the way, be it said, that at the end of his
classical studies he might be called no mean orator
or writer, though scarcely twenty years of age. But

---

[1] He was educated at the Collége Saint Louis. His father,
who was Professeur à la Faculté de Droit de Paris, and who
had kept up his classical studies with zest, superintended Henri's
education diligently.

the great, well nigh the only, event of his life was the choice of a profession. Designed by his family for the law, disposed by his own vigorous impetuosity to the military life, he was called of God to the Priest-hood; and this call, which he had recognized in childhood, and pondered during boyhood, became at eighteen his sole happiness—his only ambition. In compliance with his father's earnest wish, he went through the usual legal course, and, that ended, he came to the Oratoire in order to study philosophy and theology. His energy—not unfrequently his real courage—was severely taxed during his preparation for Orders; for when only eighteen, severe illness cast its shadow over him, and during the brief seven years of his priesthood he alternated between inexplicable attacks of serious illness and seemingly radiant health; an alternation which with him implied either the most courageous suffering, or intense, almost excessive, work. His remarkable talents in speaking and writing developed rapidly. His real power of speaking (more truly, perhaps, the real power of his mind) was proved by the wholesale, undisputed sway which he held over an audience most hard to please of any—that of the Lycée. As to his writings, the toil of those few years resulted in several volumes, precious in themselves, and full of promise for the future.

In 1860, Henri was appointed Chaplain to the
Lycée Saint Louis, where he was deeply loved, and
sorely regretted when, a year later, he was called to
the Professorship of Ecclesiastical History at the
Sorbonne. Wherever he was, carried away by the
marvellous success which everywhere fell to his lot,
he over-exerted himself, and would not learn to
husband his strength. One is forced to own that he
killed himself, like a soldier who presses to the fore-
front of the battle. Alas! for he might have lived!
he might yet be among us! Yet his death was that
of a Christian in its peaceful saintliness, its recollection
and simplicity; and his life is now eternal—a life in
which he loves and helps us yet!

Such is the brief outward history of this life, so
lovely and so short. I would strive to penetrate
somewhat into its inner beauty, ever keeping in
mind the object of so doing, namely, to stimulate
myself and others to a like noble vigour, a like moral
greatness, a like sacred devotion of life.

II.

Henri's intellectual and moral education never
ceased from childhood till death. From the first it
was a voluntary, vigorous, hearty pursuit with him;
he very early developed a strong, original will, which
was moulded by his love of beauty. A strong poetic

and religious feeling, and a taste for art—both music
and painting—filled his soul ; and, like most original
minds, he instinctively sought his point by the
simplest path, by real and natural processes ; never
by abstract rules, or the sinuosities of artificial analysis. In fact, in some of his pursuits, his originality
carried him beyond the limits of discipline. For
instance, he never would learn any of the technicali-
ties of music ; so that written music was useless to
him ; but whatever he heard, he received, retained,
and reproduced, with a meaning and feeling which
brought out all the composer's mind after a marvellous
fashion. How we used to linger, listening to that
clear, speaking touch, evening after evening ! In the
same way he drew with spirit, developing ideas with
every touch ; but without any technical knowledge.
Such details may seem insignificant, but they are
really important, because they so strikingly illustrate
a mind whose natural tendency was to follow its own
unrestrained intellectual impulses in everything, and
which nevertheless learned, as time passed on, to
submit its brilliant originality to the limits of wisdom
and rule in the fullest sense. His first progress in
intellectual culture was hindered by his absolute
repulsion, shared by so many, for abstract grammatical
study; nevertheless, he persevered in working, and
attained his end by a different way. But an

indifferent scholar in the 7th, 6th, and 5th classes, at
the Lycée Saint Louis, he was first in the catechetical
class of Saint Sulpice.   He threw himself eagerly into
this work, and through it attained the object of
secondary instruction—the arts of thinking, speaking,
and writing.   The first subjects which fixed his attention were not the weary, wordy formalism, or the set
phrases with which we are wont to exhaust the frail
understanding of children.   The first objects of
Henri's intellectual efforts were God the Father of
Heaven ; His Infinite Goodness ; His Providence ;
His Law; man's destiny ; the Son of God giving
Himself to save mankind ; the reward and blessing
promised to righteousness.   It was by such thoughts
as these that his soul was fed, and his mind strengthened : it was thus that he learnt to think, to will,
to select, to conceive, and to love that which is really
great.   It was thus side by side with a moral and
religious education that really began and developed
his intellectual education.   And I cannot but think
that it was owing to this, that, when his classical
studies ended, he had attained their object,—mental
culture,—more than most men.

Père Lacordaire, speaking of his own student life,
writes: " I was but an indifferent scholar, and had no
success in my early days . . . But suddenly a ray
broke out upon my studies in rhetoric, and before the

end of the year, a series of successes roused my
pride, more even than they rewarded my work." It
was much the same with Henri Perreyve's literary
education. One of his fellow-students says, "He
was a very poor scholar as to rhetoric, up to the 2nd
class, when, winning a small prize for Latin transla-
tion for the first time, he suddenly overstepped us all,
writing and speaking with a masterly power. He was
already well-nigh an accomplished orator and writer."
I can bear witness to this: I knew Perreyve when he
was eighteen; I watched his studies; I possess his
letters of that date, and in both the germ of coming
success was as visible as the future flower in its opening bud.

III.

I would fain apply the example of Henri Perreyve's
vigorous flight towards the greatest of all arts—that of
speaking,—to the general welfare. My duties place me
in the midst of those institutions and means, by which
a great nation, perhaps the most eloquent of modern
times, seeks to educate the flower of its youth in the
perfection of thought and speech, and I am keenly
alive to the strange and well-nigh invincible difficulties of our first processes of classical education. I
know how few minds are really brought to useful
literary study, to any real development of reason or
eloquence; unfortunately I know too, how many are

repulsed, often for ever, by an ill-advised system.   I
mean a system which undertakes to subject the child's
mind to the hard toil of an objectless study ; which
forcibly drives it from out the world of feeling and
nature in which it first springs, and for what ? To find
God, or the soul?   No ; there is some supposed
intermediate region, which is neither God, the soul,
nor nature ;—a miserable limbus, where for years the
boy is forced to dwell upon that which is purely
abstract ; to wander vaguely and without purpose
amid the empty dwelling-places where thought should
be.   If the pupil be feebly docile, if his mind be
naturally formal and one-sided, if the teacher be
unable to counteract the evil of his system by his
own vivid instructions, if the disciple be confirmed in
his groove by success and self-satisfaction, he will one
day add to that dangerous tribe of individual literary
men, with cramped intellects, who are content to
believe that the first principle is an abstract one, and
who—to cite a strange example—reduce their conception of the universe to this, "There exists naught
save formulas."   And thus we swell the numbers of
men who add to earth's misery by feeding doubt and
darkness ; who crush out the natural energy of human
thought.   Is this the rightful aim of thought and
speech ?

Well, Henri Perreyve was among the many who

refuse to subject themselves to these trammels ; and among the few who, having rejected them, attain their end by another road.

I would fain linger here, and trace lovingly the progress of that youthful mind, and the holy beauty of its first expansion. All unknowing, he followed the Saviour's call, "Suffer the little children to come unto Me." While yet a little child, he went straight to Christ through prayer and love. But that Christ is the Eternal Word, the Light Which lighteth every man that cometh into the world ;—and Henri's first intellectual efforts brought him to that Light. Philosophers tell us that in order to know the truth we must seek God, the First Cause of all intellectual life : this is what he did. Scarce knowing that it was God, he made directly for the Source of that light of which he was conscious within his soul. God, we are told, ever causes His Voice to be heard in the depth of each soul He has created ; and Henri listened for it within those depths whence truth and thought spring. Wise men tell us that the true art of education is to lead the mind to know itself, and so to pass on to know God. Henri did so, all unknowing of the maxim. He went straight to that Inner Teacher. But all the while, the External Teacher, who promulgates these maxims, too often practically disbelieves them. Far from leading minds to know themselves,

still less to know God, he hinders the disciple from
seeking God ; and if he comes across one who seeks
that inner knowledge, he generally turns him aside,
saying, as Eli said to Samuel, not perceiving God's
Voice, that it is naught ; "Lie down again, my son !"

I know that the two teachers are inseparable, and
that both should be heard ; but what are we to do
when the outer voice seeks to stifle the inner one ?
At all events, we know what is the practical result
with children. The greater number draw back, perhaps for ever, into hopeless indifference, whence
there is no rousing them. Not so dear Henri. I
watched his course, and he too drew back, for he
was quite able to defend himself against intellectual
oppression ; but there was no indifference. Already
his mind had discovered that it is better to hearken to
God than to man ; and, without understanding what
he did, his inward soul cried out with the infant
Prophet, "Speak, Lord, for Thy servant heareth !"
Yes, at twelve years old, his real, deep, habitual piety
sought inner light and the Voice of God in his own
soul, with respect, admiration, adoration. And the
result told upon him in his earliest school life : it was
the source of all his progress, for he went straight to
the Great Master. Piety, in its natural, radical sense,
means the inevitable drawing of a free, intelligent
being to his first Principle—to his Father—there to

gather renewed life : and the reason that education too often fails in its aim, the reason that it is generally so slow, so toilsome, is for lack of piety. We do not seek the Great Teacher. Our first attempts are directed towards mere words—their construction, their relation ; and no light flows from thence. The mind grovels in abstract grammatical construction, and fails to apprehend the region of thought and language. For lack of religion, the mind fails to convey meaning to the words it uses, or to reach the living soul, still less does it attain to God. Religion enables it to tread all such steps without delay, and carries it straight to God; and conversely, God speaks to the soul, the soul gives life to words, and thus real and living light are imparted.

It is thus alone that I can explain Henri's education and its success ; how at twenty, he set before us a rare example of early maturity in the art of speaking which recalled the great political orator of the last century who at twenty-three ruled the Parliament and the destiny of his country.[1] His secret was, that he gazed on and listened to God, nature, and every *chef-d'œuvre* in art, and then strove to imitate what he saw and heard. His early devotion to the First Cause of all beauty,—God—gave him the mainspring of all that is great or glorious in art, eloquence, science, or

---

[1] William Pitt.

poetry; and starting with this inner strength, he eagerly seized upon whatever of beauty came to him in outer things, and without knowing how, his own mind reproduced it in one shape or other. Thus he became an author, as he read with intense eagerness the masterpieces of ancient and modern literature :—he became an orator as he listened, trembling with enthusiasm, to that mighty voice which wielded so many hearts from the pulpit of Notre Dame—a voice Henri never ceased to follow, from the time of his First Communion. And here, by the way, let me say that he never aimed directly at being either an orator or an author,—he never wrote with a view to his own fame ;—and this total disinterestedness is the essential condition of all true and living art, such as alone is worthy of man's ambition. Henri Perreyve never spoke or wrote save from a pressing need to promote the glory and victory of that which he loved, longed for, and admired—namely, God, Who had filled his heart from childhood ; the Christian faith, which had been the stay of his youth and heart; and, next to these, justice, liberty, the welfare of mankind, the progress of nations—holy longings, which his generous, evangelic soul had conceived and grasped passionately amid the tumults of 1848.

It was in this way that he became eloquent. And herein, young men—I speak to you who are still students—you can and ought to imitate him. Do not tell me that his gifts were more the result of inherent mental riches than of any systematic excellence, and that genius cannot be imitated. I affirm, on the contrary, that every one may imitate the noble and simple line he took, from the child first beginning his studies to the man whose life is advanced and already moulded. If these pages concerning Henri Perreyve's mental history come into the hands of a child of twelve years old, that child, I say, may understand them. He can understand that the first of all teachers is God, that God Who dwells in the depth of each heart, Who ceaselessly calls forth therein both conscience and reason ;—he can perceive that God Alone gives us intelligence and a taste for work, together with a love for all that is beautiful; that these gifts must be sought from God, and that he who asks them earnestly will receive them. He can understand that all sin estranges us from God, from real work, from all beauty; that we only learn to speak and write in order to speak and write the truth : that the greatest amount of talent is useless—indeed, God often permits it to become abortive—if it is not guided by the heart ; if we do not love family, country, our brother men ; if we do not look with tender compassion upon all who suffer or go astray in the ways of misery, vice, or ignorance ; in short, if we are not firmly resolved

to devote all talent, aye, and life itself, to the
accomplishment of the utmost good within our
reach, as well as to the defence of justice and truth
with our last breath.

Of a truth it is at twelve—the age when the Child
Jesus was found among the Doctors, hearing them,
and astounding them with His questions—that these
things are comprehensible ; at forty they often cease
to be so.   Henri Perreyve did understand them at
twelve,[1] and later he taught the students of the Lycée
Saint Louis and the children whom he prepared for
their First Communion, to understand them.

IV.

To return to Henri's education.   I seem to have
ascribed to him an originality somewhat indocile—an

---

[1] In his will we find these words: "God, to Whom I had the
blessing of dedicating myself when I was twelve years old."
He was himself such a child as he describes elsewhere.   "Do you
remember the time when you were twelve ? when, for the first
time, you came to receive the Body of Jesus Christ ?   To many
men that is the most important moment of life ; a time of
angelic purity.   The mind is no longer dormant ; it is able to
see and understand ; it sees that God is Good, and that to serve
Him is to reign with Him.   Liberty is already kindled within the
heart ; but that heart is pure, and while yet unsullied with
earthborn storms, liberty is to him but a means for a nobler
obedience.   Yes, at that age, men believe in Heaven ; they are
alive to the beauty of heavenly things ; they still know how to
kneel down !"—*Discours sur l'Hist. de France.*

almost undisciplined impetuosity. In fact, it was one of his peculiarities to pass over all that is false or hollow, while he took refuge in the strongholds of intellectual conscience. He chose his own masters. and he exercised a yet further right of selection even in respect to the master chosen ; his mind was at once independent and docile. He realized that there is but One unerring Master, and He is to be found everywhere. " Call no man Master upon earth, for One is your Master, even Christ." Nevertheless, when a true word or a righteous precept touched his heart, how unbounded were his attention, his gladness, his gratitude, and interest ! How he grasped it as a gift, and made it his own for ever ! His wondrous capabilities and his magnificent intellect attracted the best teachers to him ; like—only more resolute and more docile—to that young man of whom we read in the Gospel that "Jesus, beholding him, loved him." (*"Jesus intuitus eum, dilexit eum."*) Henri won the affection of the greatest among our intellectual chieftains at the first glance, so that they spontaneously made themselves his guides ; nor did he ever forget any of their lessons. I will give an instance of what I mean from a paper in.his own handwriting, dated July, 1849. He was then seventeen, and was passing for his *baccalauréat.*

" Yesterday I was at the Luxembourg, working at physical science, and finding the work very hard, when

c

a grey-haired man, a fine specimen of venerable old age,
came up to me. He sat down beside me, and looking
stedfastly in my face, he said, ' Young man, you seem
weary of your work ; what are you reading ? ' For a
moment I was taken aback and annoyed at this unexpected interruption ; was I to lose my time listening
to a stranger's intrusive twaddle ? Oh, how thankful
I am now for that lost time ! I showed my visitor my
books ; he looked rather mournfully at them, and then
said : ' Take care how you study the natural sciences.
They are glorious if you know how to fathom them
rightly, but very dangerous if you trifle with them. A
little knowledge estranges the mind from truth and from
God ; a great deal leads it back to both. Your first
aim should be to appreciate matter, in order to realize
its beauty, its mathematical regularity, its absolute
obedience to law ; and then you must go on to learn
what a feeble thing it is after all !' He went on to
put before me a magnificent theory as to the sciences
in connection with philosophy. He spoke of the
uncertainties of Descartes and his school, of the progress of modern science, of the new inductions which
will be attempted ; with what withering contempt he
treated the coarse materialism which makes a mere
trade of intellectual speculations ! He talked about
my position and my future course. 'Success depends
upon yourself,' he said. ' Work with your whole heart.

Do not heed the world or its pleasures. If you are rich, get rid of your wealth rather than allow yourself to become absorbed in mere earthly enjoyment. It is a misfortune to be born in downright want, for want shackles the mind, and the soul suffers from being forced to devote itself to supplying the body's calls ; but it is a yet greater misfortune to be born in opulence, which may make a monarch of the body, but meanwhile makes a slave of the mind. Nothing but a revolution can save you then !' He talked about a great many other things, which I forget. I was altogether conquered by respect and admiration for the *je ne sais quoi* antique and majestic in my new friend's countenance and his white hair. At last he left me suddenly, bidding me be of good cheer, and make a right use of my youth, by devoting myself to the cause of truth. I was determined not to lose sight of him, and watched him into the Collége de France, where I found that he was M. Biot."

It was in a like manner that Henri attracted Père Lacordaire, who also took him to his heart at the first glance, and who was his teacher more than any other man, making him his son, his friend, and his heir.[1] Their friendship began when Henri was nine-

---

[1] Père Lacordaire left all that he had of personal possessions, *i.e.*, manuscripts, notes, and papers, to Henri Perreyve, thus really making him the heir of his thoughts and convictions. Perreyve

teen. For the last six years he had diligently attended the Conférences of Notre Dame, but he had never sought an introduction to the great preacher. At all times he was very reserved, and fearful of anything like presumption; perhaps, too, a lurking apprehension of falling under Lacordaire's powerful influence helped to keep him back. But at last a friend took him to see the great Dominican. The visit was of the briefest, and the good Father seemed engrossed ; but all the same he saw Henri, and that was enough. To the utter amazement and excitement of the young student, a few days later the illustrious Dominican came into his room. "*Mon enfant,*" he said, " I gave you but a sorry reception the other day. I have come to ask your forgiveness, and to have a chat with you." Thus his first lesson was one of kindness ; Henri's whole heart was won, and he speedily became Lacordaire's disciple, his son, and his friend. This lesson of kindness (*la bonté*[1]) was one often repeated by the master. Overflowing with appreciation of beauty, and love for it, Henri Perreyve had not as yet grasped the relation between benevolence and

left these documents in his turn to M. de Montalembert and M. Foisset, to be used for the "Life of Lacordaire."

[1] "Kindness" and "benevolence" fused together would most correctly render the meaning of "*bonté*;" it is not quite satisfactorily rendered by either alone.

beauty theoretically, nor had he learnt in practice
to aim at kindness to others before all else.

" I fully agree with you," Père Lacordaire wrote
to him,[1] "that beauty alone touches the depths of
the soul, but you are wrong in viewing it apart from
benevolence; there is no beauty without benevolence. Beauty implies something in which the good
and the true are harmonized, the splendour of either
melted into the other; and if you could find a face
absolutely perfect in feature and outline, but totally
wanting in some expression of benevolence about the
mouth and eyes, it would be a mere Medusa's head !
I grant that benevolence alone cannot attain to
beauty, which presupposes a certain degree of splendour; and in this sense benevolence alone does not
dazzle the eyes." So much for the speculative side
of the question. In another letter the Father gives
a personal, practical lesson on the same subject.[1] " I
hope to see you one day what you promise to be,
a useful, honourable, distinguished man. You will
have to shun certain snares, and there is the material
for many faults within you, but I think and hope
they will be of a generous kind, such as God forgives—
I was going to say loves—generosity is so precious
in His sight ! During the last four years I have seen
many things which have disgusted me with men.

[1] " Lettres à des Jeunes Gens," LVI.

You abide in an unsullied hope of a bright future ; but if you would be stable, be temperate. Impetuosity and exaggeration often lead to strange backslidings, whereas temperate thoughts and actions do not find it hard to abide firm. Above all things be kind; kindness makes us like to God, and disarms men. You have traces thereof in your soul, but we rarely cut these furrows deep enough. Your lips and your eyes are not yet as benevolent as they might be, and no act can give them this stamp save the inward cultivation of a kind spirit. Gentle, kindly thoughts of others in time leave their impress upon the countenance, and set a mark upon it which wins all hearts. I never felt affection where there was a total deficiency of kindness in a person's face. Everything short of that chills me, even those heads which are most full of genius. But any one whatsoever who gives one an impression of benevolence touches and wins me."[1]

The disciple was not hard to convince on this score, and later on he commended, as the true and definitively philosophical analysis of beauty, these words concerning the human face : " Even as science detects three component rays in daylight, so must beauty possess the three indispensable rays—courage, intelligence, and benevolence. The lack of either

[1] " Lettres à des Jeunes Gens," XLI.

of the three destroys beauty ; their combination produces it."

Assuredly he himself possessed them all, and his life was but the development of these rays. In the order of nature courage was the most prominent in him, then intelligence, lastly benevolence ; but by grace and culture he developed that above all else, and devoted his whole courage and intelligence to the love of his fellow-creatures. One may truly say that he "increased in grace and loving kindness, and in favour with God and man," to his last hour. And there was such truthfulness, such frankness and purity in that growth ! Most assuredly he never studied to acquire beauty of expression, or to show forth in eyes and lips the benevolence of which Père Lacordaire spoke. All that is artificial and a matter of calculation was equally foreign to his mind and to his countenance. But real goodness, like real love, consists mainly in the absence of all self-concentration, in the hearty throwing of oneself into a higher aim. And Henri Perreyve threw himself most heartily into his work, into his duty, into the welfare of man and the service of God. This lesson he learned from God Himself during the severe training of a repeated prospect of death—a prospect which came before him at eighteen, at twenty-three, and at twenty-six, to say nothing of the final preparation. "The habit of being

ill and of thinking of death " (he wrote, Aug. 23rd,
1855), "has given me a tendency to love my fellow-
creatures. Perhaps it does not affect everybody in
the same way, but it seems to me that life being the
brief, fragile thing that it is, at all events we should
not spend it in hating one another ; and inasmuch
as death dogs our heels at every step, one should
strive to hold oneself ready to leave the world *en ami.*
However, it is not hard for me to love mankind ; I
should be detestably ungrateful if I did anything else.
Day by day I am amazed at the amount of kindness,
goodwill, and friendship shown me by unknown
people, and if anything troubles me in the matter,
it is the feeling of my own unworthiness of so much
kindness."

Perhaps, however, nothing sets forth so plainly the
loving kindness which had been wrought in his soul
by the contemplation of death face to face, as his
own words concerning the Return to Life,[1] where he
makes the Divine Master say, " My son, it is not for
thine own sake that thou hast received the renewed
gift of life. This life now restored to thee, thou
owest it to thy fellow-men for My Glory's sake. The
close approach of death throws a vivid light upon
the extreme simplicity of life—detail vanishes, nought
remains visible to the soul save the salvation of

[1] "Le Retour à la Vie." "Journée des Malades."

mankind and God. Such, my son, is the sacred teaching of death. Blessed are those souls who, having tasted thereof, on their return to life do not remember it in vain!"

It was when eighteen that Henri Perreyve received this teaching of death for the first time, and he returned to life fully understanding, fully remembering it. He returned to life having made up his mind advisedly and deliberately to follow Jesus Christ as His servant only, and to give his life for man's salvation and the Glory of God.

CHAPTER II.

VOCATION.

I.

I SAID that the great act, the only event of Henri Perreyve's life was the choice of his career. But indeed I should not have used the word *choice*, for in truth it was not a choice. His priestly vocation was unquestionable ; unhesitating from the time he was twelve years old, untroubled by one passing regret to his last hour. He never conceived the possibility of any other purpose in life. He looked upon the Priesthood as incomparably the highest, noblest, most useful and most beautiful path that man can follow on earth. He thought that above all now, when Europe and the whole world are passing through such perilous vicissitudes, it was the time for the noblest hearts and most powerful minds to enlist in God's army. While but a mere boy he urged these truths upon those he loved, and, thanks be to God, " he being dead yet speaketh," and will long speak not only by his example, but by the sacred fire which bursts out in his letters and writings. The marvels of God's doings are to be found, indeed, in all souls drawn by Him to the ministry of His Gospel, however humble warriors of heaven they may be; but it is yet more striking to trace these marvels in a soul so full of poetry, intelligence and enthusiasm as was Henri Perreyve's.

The first words of his will are: "I die in the bosom of the Catholic Church, to the service of which I had the happiness of devoting myself at twelve years of age." And at the end of his life he said, "If it should please God to recall me to life, I would fain enter more deeply into the spirit of the Priesthood." At one-and-twenty he wrote: "I do not remember to have felt a single real doubt as to my vocation for the last eight or nine years."

The following letter, written the day before he received Deacon's Orders, to the priest who gave him his first Communion, tells how that vocation arose; how it sprang, so to say, from two separate roots; that virgin piety which turns to God out of love, and that clear sight and manly courage which, gazing upon the bitterness of human suffering and the terrible struggle between good and evil set before us by this world, hastens to become God's soldier, and enthusiastically pledges itself to combat until death in His Cause.

"You know that I always trace God's earliest call to me, as regards my vocation, to my first Communion. It is a thought most precious to me. I can recall, as if it were but yesterday, the sacred moment when, having just received our Lord, I returned from the altar to my place, and there kneeling on that bench covered with red velvet (I see it now!) I promised our Dear Lord, with an impulse of most sincere love, to be His for ever, His only. Even now I can recall the sort of certainty which came over me at the time that I was accepted; I feel the warmth of those tears, the first to fall from my child-eyes for the love of Jesus, and the ineffable bewilderment of a soul which has spoken to God, has seen and heard Him for the first time. Precious, hidden joys of a sacred betrothal! With what respect and love I cherish this remembrance, now that God has vouchsafed to confirm His promises, and to let me realize the longing of those childish days! Dear sir, dear friend, can you understand that this sweet remembrance has kindled a feeling which I can only call *la superstition de la première Communion?* I feel as if almost one's whole life depended on that day, as if on that day one entered into a final pact with God, as if then, as a dear little child of twelve lately said to me, one pledged one's whole eternity. Blessed and memorable day!

You had your share in it, dear sir ; God made use of you to bring it about, and I shall be grateful to you for all eternity. Let me, though not for the last time, express once more my gratitude as well as my respectful and affectionate friendship."

The secret of this vocation, however, remained hidden in Henri's heart until, at the age of nineteen, it was revealed to one of his dearest and most intimate friends.

"Florence, May 18th, 1850.

" So you too feel the need for a more complete self-devotion, a more entire sacrifice ? you too have found out that in the times in which our lot is cast, only those men will be useful who freely accept the task of self-denial and combat ? You too have heard that voice which they hear whom God has chosen, when He assigns to each his post ! It has pleased Him to enlist you too in the army He is making ready for the coming strife ! Indeed I thank you for confiding this to me, and while so doing, I must also make a confession. The only secret I ever kept from you is just this very thing which you have told me so frankly. Ever since I was a child the thought of being a priest has been in my heart; not at all times equally prominent, but never absent. This year, or rather the last two years, it has been stronger, and during the visit to the Apostle's tomb which I have been lately

permitted to make I made the final offering of my life
to my master's service. I have prayed that God would
make me such as He would have me to be, for His
greater Glory, and the service of our brethren ; I have
sworn to renounce all that we call rest, happiness, this
world's interests, in order to accept a life of toil
and struggle. Shall I have strength to do so ? I
know not, but I hope it, for in God alone is my
strength.

"What better object for one's life in these times than
to fight for all the truths which are at stake ! or were
there ever more just causes for self-devotion ? or
rather, one could say, a more just cause, for all else is
gathered up into God's Cause ! How many things
will ere long be decided either by the sword or by
words ; in either case by strife ! Oh, do not let us
fall out of our ranks in this new war ; let us take a
bold stand, for we have come into the world in a
season destined by God to witness many a disruption
and many a sorrow."

A few days later Henri replied to another letter
from the same friend by the following urgent advo-
cacy of the priestly vocation. Remembering the age
of the writer, one can but marvel at the wisdom, the
dignity and ripe thought it sets forth—one omission
excepted—the sacredness of Christian marriage, upon
which he does not touch.

" Florence, June 6th, 1851.[1]

" MY DEAR FRIEND—I have just received your letter of May 30, which says that you had already written a few days before. I am very sorry to have lost that letter, in which probably you spoke of your new resolutions and the state of your mind. As far as I can guess from this note, you are agitated and even distressed, and it grieves me not to be at hand to drive away your gloomy thoughts, and shake you up, if need be, with my nonsense ! But I will not delay answering your question ; it is serious, and rather alarming. You say, " Do you think me such as God requires His servants to be ? Am I fit for the priestly office ? Have I a vocation ? " I will answer you with all the frankness, all the sincerity which my affection for you demands. And first of all, dear friend, I would say, that of all conditions of life, I should say one requiring courage and self-devotion is best suited to the needs and tendencies of your soul. I believe that with your sensitiveness, and abhorrence of the *vilaineries* of men,

[1] Henri Perreyve went to Rome in 1850, after his first serious illness. He returned there again 1855, and it was at Rome, in San Giovanni in Laterno, that he received subdeacon's orders, May 17, 1856. He was yet once again there, 1857, in company with his dear friend Père Adolphe Perraud, and it was during a retreat he attended before quitting Rome this last time that he wrote the " Meditations " quoted further on.

you would not be happy in the world. The precious
things of this world are not what men generally
suppose them to be ; so far as I have seen they are
full of cruel delusions. Ambition, love of ease and
rest, the pride of talent, even the desire for average
attainment, continually fall short of their aim, which
few men reach. Even the purest affections of the
heart are often turned to bitterness. In short, I believe
that happiness is a very rare thing, if by happiness we
mean an easy, pleasant, honourable life. On the
other hand, it seems to me a wise thing, and to those
souls who are thus led by God an easy thing, to seek
somewhat better than these poor passing joys, to overcome the passions which deceive us, and from the
beginning to renounce illusions which must be given up
sooner or later. Your mind is of sufficiently high
stamp to make short work of all these troubles. I do
not see that those around us who have followed after
this world's joys have found real happiness ; they
are restless, anxious, and in the present uncertainty,
with the prospect of fierce strife ahead, they have not
even that last resource of the hour of danger—power
to make a free sacrifice. And so they are perturbed to
the very depths of their hearts, feeling the ground in
which they have sown all their hopes to be giving
away beneath them. Happy they who, when freedom
and activity become necessary, are not clogged

with the things of this world ! Nor can I see, my
dear Charles, that it is so hard to preserve this precious independence. I do not want you to die to the
world. I want you to live in it, but in freedom ! I
cannot see the horrors of self-sacrifice, if one escapes
from slavery !

"I dwell the more on my belief that you may find happiness, and that very real, in the priestly office, because
I think that D——'s letter which you sent me rather
exaggerates the severe and dismal side of such a deter-
mination. The love of God is much more fully carried
out by life than by death. Profane love often causes
men to die to good things and noble impulses, but
God's Love kindles and gives life to all ; it destroys the
germs of death which evil times have cast within the
soul ; it redoubles a man's strength, because it leaves
him only that which is immortal. Do take hold of the
belief that, especially in these times in which we live,
whoever acts vigorously in behalf of truth and the good
of his fellow men proves his hearty love of God. From
this point of view your heart, with its longings for all
that is noble, will find rest in fulfilling the Divine Will.
I believe you to be specially capable of detachment
from this world's little pleasures, and of the thorough,
hearty, continual self-devotion of a free mind to the
happiness of one's brother men and the Glory of God.

"I am very sorry to seem to contradict what D——

D

says. I know that he is far ahead of me in goodness :
there are the elements of a saint in him. I both love
and respect him, for most certainly he is worth far
more than me in the mysterious scales of human
virtue. But I cannot refrain from saying that I think
he carries certain principles too far. It seems to me
that the famous saying, that we are to be as a staff or
a corpse in God's Hand, [1] can only tend to revolt the
heart, inasmuch as it is opposed to reason, which is

[1] I know Henri Perreyve's mind, its habitual wisdom and
modesty, too well not to be certain that in these words he does
not mean to condemn the old maxim "*perinde ac cadaver*," or the
"*sicut lignum aut lapis*" of the Dominican and other rules : if
nothing else, his respect for Père Lacordaire would have hindered
this. Nor would his bold judgment, passed when nineteen, be
very important. But I do not think that he meant this. He
was well aware that these maxims of absolute obedience, understood and applied as they are in religious orders, subject to the
Church's interpretation, are as true, as necessary, and as noble
as those rules of military obedience, which enable us to lead
whole armies like an individual mass to meet death. What
Henri rightly condemned is the abuse, at once absurd and
dangerous, too often made of these maxims, which are only
applicable to obedience in a religious order, or in an army
(*obéissance réligieuse*, or *obéissance militaire*). He found fault
with that spurious devotion, which is destructive to all reason
and moral liberty, and which Bossuet calls "*anéantissement
pervers ;*" a system of, or rather an abuse of direction such as I
have seen, which seeks to impose passive obedience on the part
of a penitent to his director ; an abuse which is pointed out and
condemned by all the true masters of the interior life.

God's own gift. Our religion does not exact any such
thing of her ministers, nor are our mysteries so absurd
as to require a man to renounce sense and reason in
order to love them. For my own part, I confess that
if that is perfection, I am not only very far from it, but
I do not even aspire to its attainment. God has often
spoken to my soul, but He has never bidden it abdi-
cate its functions so far as to renounce all knowledge
of what it says or does, in order to live solely in His
thought or action. Take my advice, and do not give
too much weight to such words which spring from
D——'s own enthusiastic self-devotion, and which are
unsuitable for neophytes. Consult enlightened men,
who know more of the real, downright side of the
priestly life than D—— can know. The Abbé G——
could tell you a thousand times more than any of us
can. Such men, I am sure, would tell you that one is
no less a man when one becomes a Priest, and that
one is free to speak, act, reason and think even after
one has devoted one's life to the service of mankind
for the love of our Common Father. Were it otherwise, Christian life would be alarming, not merely as
seen from the side of human weakness, but also from
that of human dignity; whereas I believe it to be fearful only to our weakness. Let me dwell somewhat on
this thought, because I think it must be echoed in
your heart. I am certain that you have felt most

unworthy of such an undertaking. You have confessed yourself weak, deficient in worth, little trained in virtue, and you have naturally asked yourself how, with all your spiritual poverty, you could presume to approach Him Who cast into outer darkness the man who had not on a wedding garment. I must confess that I am often so disturbed at the thought of my own infirmities as to be well nigh discouraged. Indeed, dear friend, I am bad in many ways—very bad. I make this confession (as many another) in order to strengthen you in hope and trust, you whom I know to be better and farther on than I am. Nevertheless I have not lost hope, and I trust in God, ' Who lifteth the poor out of the mire, that He may set him among princes,' that He will at last hear my prayers, and will heal me when I have called out long enough, ' Jesus, Thou Son of David, have mercy upon me !' like the blind man who sat by the wayside. Think, then, whether you ought not to be trustful, if I do not despair ; if, notwithstanding all the weakness and contradictions and cowardice which you know exist in me, I can dare to say, ' I mean to be a Priest.' Is it a mistake of mine ? Am I insane on this subject of the future ? Is the voice I have so often seemed to hear a mere illusion ? I reject the idea as a temptation of the Evil One. Hoping everything from Him Who could save the world with one drop

of His Blood, I persist, and I am resolved to persist,
in drawing near to Him. His help will not be
wanting. This thought, which has often comforted
and reassured me, ought to reassure you too, and
prevent you from looking upon the priestly calling in
a light so difficult and repulsive to a noble mind
as might possibly lead you to despise the gracious
inspiration of God to a soul He loves. Unquestionably
the grand work is serious, solemn, from some points
of view severe. One must give up all common pleasures, all worldly festivities ; but do we care very much
about them ? We must give up the charms of ambition ; but among many ambitious men how few are
satisfied ? One gives up family happiness ; but remember how S. Francis de Sales defines marriage as
an order, wherein, were there a year's novitiate, but
few would be professed ! Nor do our natural affections forsake us because one has given up one's life
to holier, graver objects. Why should I love you less,
why should those who know you care less for you,
because your devotion to them has less interested
motives than formerly ? Will you care less for study,
books, meditation ? Will there be no more poetry,
no more imagination for you, because you have drawn
nearer to the Source of all poetry and of noble imagi-
nations ? Are you to lose your place and your rights
in society, because you are more wholly devoted to

its welfare? Will you be less a citizen of your own
country, less a lover of liberty, less eager after coming
improvements, because you have become the servant
of Him Who made all men alike? because your life
is shaped upon that Gospel which is the code of all
progress? Or again;—Will you forfeit the talents
which God has given you, because you have consecrated them to His service Who is the First Principle of all intelligence, the Dispenser of all virtues?
Assuredly not. The sacrifice which is required of us
is that which humbles and abases us daily, our continual hesitation and stumbling between good and
evil; all those little clingings to self-estimation which
are the torment of one's life, and which make one
both unhappy and ridiculous; that vice of luxury
which at nineteen unnerves our hearts by its very
name, which is the enemy of all that is great, of all
courage, of all moral independence. This is the
sacrifice God requires of us: this it is which I must
tear from my soul at so severe a cost, and lay it at
the foot of the Cross. What else can I say to you,
save the words which God seems to put into my
mouth, that they may reach you with a friend's
authority: Courage and confidence! I would that
I were disposed, like you, to a severe life of self-
devotion! But it may come; it will come with
God's Help.

"Yet once more, dear friend, do not be afraid of the Cross. How heavy soever it be, it does not weary men so much as the voluptuousness of life! Take it up, or rather let us take up and carry together that ensign which has been and will be the token of the triumph of goodness, justice, and truth. I would not be the first to speak to you of my intentions, because I know how impressionable you are, and I felt that, if such thoughts were ever to come to you, there should be no interference between your heart and God. Now I think you must be glad of this reserve, for your resolution has been wholly independent, and my only share therein lies in the prayers that I have offered to God, and in the gladness with which my affection for you now fills me. I was about to break through the irksome constraint of a secret between us two, when Providence was beforehand with me. I am most thankful; and, not having suggested the idea, I have the better right to urge you to follow it; and so I have indulged to-day in this urgent advice."

II.

To another dear friend, who about this time decided on following the sacred calling of the Priesthood, Henri wrote with a delight and trust which overflow in a sort of ecstasy :

"July 1st, 1851.

"I cannot keep quiet; the tidings which H——
has told me, or which, perhaps more truly, I have
guessed, fill me with joy. I don't know whether I
have any right to say anything about it to you, before you have told me yourself. But never mind:
forgive or blame me as you may, I must embrace you
as a brother in our Lord Jesus Christ—that is to say,
with all the love and tenderness possible. I cannot
sufficiently marvel at the way God orders things. He
drew us together in the bonds of friendship before committing His work to us. We had but one
heart before we aspired to the same vocation, and
therein we became really members of the same family,
even as men speak of such things; and it needed but
that God's Will should be made plain to one of us,
for light to break forth in hearts so closely bound
together.

" Courage, then, most happy friend. Our vocations
are bound up together with yours. You are but the
first of a daily swelling cohort. We congratulate you
as one congratulates the foremost, the first to touch
the goal; we triumph in your progress, and take part
in it with pride, because your victory is ours, and we
are dedicated with you. No doubt you tremble, you
are sad, perhaps even you may weep in your inner
heart; but do not take such shrinking to be hesitation.

You do not hesitate; I know your mind, you have no lack of firmness, and irresolution will never trouble you much. It seems to me that this depression is no more than that remarkable sensation which always comes across one on the eve of any important event in life, a shrinking from which the greatest happiness is not exempt. Believe me, this is your case. Our poor human nature fears all that greatly moves it, and weeps out of sheer weakness, even when it is God's Own Hand that touches it. Take courage, be strong, and do not take that to be real hesitation which is merely the failing of a heart overpowered by its own gift of grace, yielding beneath the weight of very happiness. Kings have been known to weep on their coronation day; and you, as you take the first step on the royal road, feel somewhat of the like overwhelming sensation. Never mind, our pride and joy will help to reassure you. I gaze on you from afar, and intreat the Lord to give you inward strength to bear the burden of so great a dignity. Adieu. All my heart and all my trust are with you. Some day, when the dull routine of life sinks down upon me again, I shall come to you to be cheered under my weakness: to-day I can do nothing but raise a song of thanksgiving!

"Ever your devoted in Jesus Christ."

Let us turn next with loving reverence to the

earnest outpouring of Henri's heart to his dear friend,
Charles Perraud, who was about to celebrate his first
mass :

"Hyères,[1] December 16th, 1857.

"The Lord be with you. These are the sacramental words of the deacon, the only words that I
have any right to say to you, dear friend and brother,
as you go up to the holy Altar. But I say them out
of the very fulness of my heart, and with all the
deepest meaning such solemn words convey. Yes,
indeed, may the Lord be with you, dear brother !
May He be with you this morning at the altar of
your first mass, to accept your virgin troth, and to
receive your eternal vows with that reciprocal love
which exceeds all other love.

"May He be with you all through this great day,
to preserve within your soul that perfume of heavenly
incense, that sweet scent of the sacrifice you have
begun, but which, thank God, knows no end. May
He be with you to-morrow, to teach you that His
joy possesses a somewhat eternal, which, unlike earth's
joys, can never be exhausted. May He be with you
when, the first sacred intoxicating delight over, you
realize that it is yours to minister to men, and that

---

[1] Henri Perreyve spent the winter of 1857--58 at Hyères with
the Père Gratry, and it was while there that he resolved on
joining the little company of the Oratoire de France.

you must leave Mount Tabor, and seek the suffering, the ignorant, those who hunger and thirst for the true light and life. May He be with you in your grief to comfort you; in your joy to sanctify you; in all your longings, that they may bring forth fruit. ' *Memor sit omnis sacrificii tui, et holocaustum tuum pingue fiat!* '

" May He be with you, dear Charles, if you are alone in life, if our friendship is soon cut short, if you are left to lean only on your Divine Friend. May He be with you as a young priest; with you when grown old amid the struggles of the priesthood, in the service of God and man. May He be with you in the hour of death, when some other hand will bring to your lips that Same Jesus Whom even now your own trembling hand has laid there. Oh, dear friend, I sum up all that my heart can hold of longings, hopes, prayers for you with the intreaty, ' May the Lord be ever with you.' That, indeed, will assure the life of a holy priest here, and hereafter Heaven itself. ' The Lord be with you.'

" Dearest Charles, give me your blessing. I embrace you lovingly, and feel as though drawn with you close to the Heart of our Ever Dear and Blessed Master.

" HENRI PERREYVE."

III.

What was this bold energy with which Henri moved
—urged his friends to the priestly office ; this enthusiastic confidence which prompted him to bid the
shrinking go on, to tell the sad that their heart fails
but from the very excess of joy? Was it an imprudent enthusiasm? No : to me it seems rather a deep
wisdom, a bright inspiration ; and I draw therefrom a
lesson which we all greatly need.

I affirm that one great hindrance to the world's
good is that whereas men rush into all possible
careers, save one, with unhesitating confidence, for
the most part they shrink back with gloomy fear from
the priesthood. I affirm that many men go hence
after a useless life, who might have used their great
and plenteous mental gifts on behalf of their brethren,
if they had but known how to devote their lives to
God. If anything in the world is an obvious fact, it
is that we want a thousand times more men who are
devoted to the religious and moral instruction of the
human race. All the world over, incalculable moral
wealth is lost for lack of labourers in the harvest of
souls. "The harvest truly is great, but the labourers
are few." And this lack of real labourers is one of
the characteristics of the history of the world in this
present age ; consequently, almost all work, without

exception, is behindhand. "Pray ye, therefore, the
Lord of the harvest, that He would send forth
labourers into His harvest." This is the foremost
need of the world we live in: this it is we must ask
of God.

Truly, I know no wiser enthusiasm than that which
stimulates men to become labourers for God.

We have too few priests; we have far too many
soldiers. No man becomes a priest whether he will
or no; but on all sides the strong hand of the powers
that be constrains men by thousands to be soldiers
whether they will or no. Why is the priest's lot to be
counted worse than the soldier's? He who chooses
the sacred toil of God's harvest field for his life's
labour, chooses the better part. Surely his ambition
is beyond all comparison the greatest, best, and
noblest; his work the most fruitful, the most necessary. That is but a sorry delusion by which the
world would set the priesthood before men as in the
shadow of death, and other careers in a glow of light,
life, and glory.

But some will say, may a man not well hesitate
before entering upon a life-long engagement, and has
it never happened that a soul which was pledged
under the excitement of youthful enthusiasm has
experienced mortal regrets under the irreparable
sacrifice?

Well, let us look this living sacrifice to God's service, whether in the priesthood or the religious life,
steadily in the face. The thought thereof is as overwhelming as death to the world; to a man's family,
his friends : it may be that at intervals it sweeps
with terror even over the heart which can appreciate
its beauty. Friends cry out that he is lost to them !
How, they ask, will it be if, in the midst or at the
end of his career, he should find that he was mistaken?
Has it never happened to priests or religious to be
driven in their heart to make the terrible confession :
" The ardour of youthful piety has plunged me for
ever into an abyss of which I knew nothing ! Enthusiasm deceived me !" I grant that some such there
have been. But, first of all, I would ask whether such
deception, such regrets, are peculiar to the priesthood
and the religious life, or whether they are not to be
met with in every other walk of life—in the soldier's
life, even in many a home ?

Let us take an example. A young fellow of twenty
leaves the Military School of Saint Cyr, brimming
over with energy and impetuous courage. A month
later, burning with enthusiasm, he rushes into his
first battle ; he is wounded : he lies, it may be a day,
it may be more, untended. At length comes a tardy
amputation, and the next day he is carried forth from
the ambulance, dead. I have known such : you who

read have all known such. Thousands have died thus.
Now, think of that lad lying on the battle-field, amid
the dying and the dead, enduring a martyrdom as
bitter as that of any missionary. A cavalry regiment
sweeps over him : he is miraculously spared ; a train
of artillery follows, and he is wounded afresh. For
hours he lies in a semi-stupor amid the roar of
cannon, from which he is roused by the succeeding
silence. He would fain tell the time. At length he
realizes that the day is well nigh spent, that night is
coming ; and then all hope of succour is past. And
what then ? Alas ! we know it too well. His heart
yearns over his mother, the dear ones at home, the
life hitherto slighted. He cries out to them, either
aloud or within his heart, with a bitterness no words
can tell. And vague thoughts cross his failing mind
—" Enthusiasm and glory . . . military tales and
poetry, gay uniforms ! . . . and here we are, perhaps
some thirty thousand, writhing on the bare earth in
agony ! For what have I given my life ? for my
mother, or my country ? . . . Why will men kill one
another ? How long is mutual slaughter to be a
public institution ? To what end the heroic courage
of those two hundred thousand men who even now
rushed to death as to a festival ? It is not for this
that God gave us life. . . . We have been deceived
by high-flown words. . . . We have been fooled by

the world's treachery. . . . Empty enthusiasm has whirled us on like straws upon the wind. . . . And after all—here we are ! . . . and this will go on, and others will fall like me !" In all sad truth I ask, how many European soldiers have died with some such thoughts in their hearts during the last few years?[1] We must count them, assuredly, by hun-

---

[1] Alas and alas ! for this was written before Sadowa, before the Prussian war, before France was steeped in blood by the hands of her own children, as well as by those of strangers ! The Abbé Gratry refers to the "Souvenirs de Solferino"— souvenirs, alas ! now well nigh effaced under the more terrible memories of the present year. Yet, unhappily, there is but too fearful a family likeness in all cases among battle-fields. Let us listen to "The Day after a Battle." "The rising sun of the 25th lights up as awful a scene as imagination can conceive. The battle-field strewn with corpses of men and horses,—roads, ditches, ravines, thickets, meadows all strewed with dead bodies,—the shores of Solferino thick with them. Fields trodden down, corn and maize crushed, hedges torn up, orchards destroyed. Here and there pools of blood,—the ground covered with guns, knapsacks, shakos, belts, helmets, kepis, arms ! All through the day wretched sufferers are carried away, pale, livid, aghast. Some of the most mutilated are stupefied, and scarcely seem to understand what one says ; they only fix their haggard eyes upon you, but they suffer all the same ! Others are restless, and shiver convulsively ; others again, almost wild with the pain of gaping wounds wherein inflammation has set in, cry out to be set free from their woes, and writhe in helpless agony. Then, again, there are the poor wretches who have not only been wounded by shell or ball, but whose limbs have also been broken by the artillery trains passing over them. Cylindrical balls have smashed the bones of others, conical balls have

dreds of thousands. And during that period of time
how many priests, think you, have discovered that
they were the victims of a delusion? Could you
venture to reckon them at a hundred? What of the

wrought all manner of horrible internal injuries; and such
wounds are hideously aggravated by splinters of bone, accoutre-
ment, lead, or other extraneous matter, forced in and adding
torture to the gash. At every step you meet despair and
anguish, tossed together amid the wildest confusion. . . . .
Among the dead, some who have been instantaneously killed
present a calm aspect, but the greater part are contorted with
agony, their limbs stiffened, their hands clenched, or griping
the earth, their moustache raised, a horrible convulsive grin
displaying the teeth. Three days and nights were spent in
burying the bodies which lay on the battle-field, but numbers
who were hidden in ditches or furrows, concealed by thickets or
undulating ground, were not found till much later, and the fœtid
odour from these, as well as from the dead horses, was intolerable.
One fears that some yet living must have shared the grave of the
really dead. Here is a son, his parents' idol, brought up and
cared for during so many years by a mother who trembled if he
did but look pale ; there a well known officer, who left wife and
children at home ; a youth who has quitted father and mother,
sister and fiancée, stretched in dust and mud, bathed in blood,
scarce to be recognized,—sabre and *mitraille* have not spared him.
He has borne his pangs, he dies, and the fondly cherished body,
now black, swollen, and hideous, will be hastily tossed as it is
into a scarcely finished grave—a few spadefuls of lime and
earth scarce sufficing to hide the remains from the carrion birds,
who are quick to espy a hand or foot pushing through the
sodden earth. By-and-by a little more earth will be thrown
down—perhaps a wooden cross may be erected, and that is all.
. . . . What sufferings, what agony during the 25th, 26th,

E

legions of *réligieuses*, whose numbers increase daily?
They know why they live, and they know, too, why
they die, when they sink beneath their toil among
the poor, not seldom on the field of battle, or in the
hospital. They know why — they know that it is

and 27th ! Wounds became irritated with the heat and dust,
and the lack of water or care, mephitic vapour poisoned the air,
in spite of all praiseworthy efforts of officials, — an insufficient
staff of *infirmiers* and nurses became cruelly pressed, as fresh
convoys poured in their contingents of wounded. Here is a
soldier hopelessly disfigured, whose tongue hangs out from his
torn jaw. I can but steep a handful of lint in the pail carried
by, and squeeze some water from this improvised sponge into the
shapeless hole which should be a mouth. There is another
poor fellow part of whose face has been carried away by a sabre
cut—nose, lips, and chin severed—speech is impossible to him,
and he can scarcely see—with heart-rending gesticulations and
guttural sounds he attracts one's attention ; one can give him
drink, and sprinkle water upon his bleeding face. Another, his
skull split open, dies as he is laid within the church's aisle—his
fellow sufferers kick him aside because he cumbers the passage.
I can but shield his last moments, and cover the poor quivering
head with a handkerchief. Some there are who cry out that
they cannot die ! and expire as they make the last effort of
nature. One young corporal, with a fine expressive face,
Claude Mazuet by name, lies hopelessly wounded with a ball in
his left side. He knows his state and thanking one for giving him
drink, adds, '*Ah, Monsieur*, if you could write to my father and
tell him to comfort my mother !' I took the address, and he was
gone ! An old sergeant, with several decorations, said with deep
sadness and with the most thorough conviction : ' If I had been
sooner tended, I might have lived, but as it is I shall be dead
before night ;' and he was dead before night."

in order to save their poor wounded brethren by hundreds from despair and death.

You parents, who mourned over your child as though she were dead, when she became the bride of Christ, refusing the husband you desired for her, do you know the secret thoughts of that man's actual wife? Alas! too often I have had to hear such. "If those young girls who have as yet not left their mother's side knew what I know, and the revelations which come upon so many of us, there would not be convents enough in the world to receive those who would fly from the possibility of so much sorrow." Yes, there are hundreds who wake too late to find that they have been the victims of youthful enthusiasm, under the fascinating garb of love, within the sacred pale of family life. No doubt such cases are more rare than the soldier's bitter awakening, but, depend upon it, they are far more common than regrets among the brides of Christ or the soldiers of God's army. What conclusion are we to draw from this? Would you abolish family ties, or disband the army?[1] Surely not; but we must grant that there are disappointments everywhere, specially in quarters

[1] Mgr. d'Orléans, in his funeral oration upon General Lamoricière, exclaims: "Of a truth I deplore the sorrowful mystery of war, and I daily pray that it may be withheld, abolished if possible. But while deploring the horrors of war, who does not admire the army?"

least perceived by the world.   In truth, on all sides
we find sacrifice ; and that which is altogether hopeless and crushing is the sacrifice which brings naught
save horror, where men look for glory and happiness.

IV.

Meanwhile, the lesson I would draw from this is
that both courage and love may be otherwise employed.   Far be it from me to wish to lessen among
us either that courage which goes forth to face death
or that love on which family ties are founded.   On
the contrary, both should be strengthened ; pointed
to their highest aim ; transfigured.   And what is
capable of doing this, save evangelic sacrifice, sacerdotal sacrifice which transfigures all things?

Surely that heroic courage with which God has so
deeply endowed many men will not always find its
sole or main outlet in killing the choicest among our
brethren !   The savage recognizes one only occupa-
tion worthy of man—war.   But we who are shaking
off barbarism, in thought at least, we know something
better.   The spirit of our age is rising to a conception
that war should diminish and work increase !   We
are becoming wise enough to realize that no nation
possesses more than sufficient strong, young, brave,
noble-hearted men to combat against misery and
hunger, ignorance and vice, sickness and spoiling

waste—that never-ending tribe of evils. Yet there is a higher perception still, which realizes the cause of all these woes; which perceives that the earth is covered with blood and tears, because men know neither God nor their own souls, neither virtue, truth, nor love. It sees, overwhelmingly, that the grandest use of life and courage lies in daring all things, even death itself, in order to enlighten men, to shield them from the fury of oppression, spoliation, mutual destruction; to lead them, if it may be, to justice, union, and loving kindness; to break the Satanic fetters which bind the human race.

He who lives and dies in this cause has no doubt, when his last hour comes, for what it is that he has lived. From the first he knew that life is very short, that it must needs be sold at a high price, and that it befits us ever to aim at that which is highest, most useful, most beautiful. And if any one among us has early grasped a view of our globe's existing condition the origin of our habits, the root of our difficulties, and the source of our strength, he will see, as in the brightest sunlight, how urgent is the need, and, thanks be to God, how great is the possibility of a mighty progress in the human race. But at the same time he will see that the world is in a hard strait, and that the main duty to-day of thoughtful men is to turn aside from all else, in order to employ all their courage and strength in a vigorous effort to set forward through intense self-devotion and energy the perilous course of that mighty vessel, freighted as she is with the human race.

Only imagine what would be the addition to the world's strength and her resources if there were found among us more of what I must call the *transformation of courage!* If only all the strength, the science, the courage, the genius, the heroism, the brave blood expended in one great battle could be used in accordance with the knowledge and inspiration of God, it would, I believe, transform the whole world ! What if all that immense noble force we call military courage were devoted, not to the extermination of men, but, as God would have it, in a fearless, devoted contest with the endless woes which overwhelm mankind? Is there no need throughout the globe, beginning at home, to put an end to a purely savage, barbarous life? Are there not yet among us monsters, tyrants, who shed blood even as men tread out the grapes? Is there no need to train up free men all through the world? Are there not barren, pestiferous districts, whence a deadly miasma ever breathes destruction? Are there no dangerous beasts, no still more dangerous men to conquer? Is it not a seemly task for noble hearts to strive and overcome, not by mere force, but by education and renovation, those mortal foes of justice and peace which are broadcast in every land? Does not every nation need the bravest vigilance to watch over those ever rising spectres of oppression and destruction? What of the firm, unwavering struggle we needs must undertake against the invincible scourge of want, that exterminating evil which mows down the weak on all sides, and binds down one third of the human race to suffering and scalding tears for life? What of the yet more needful, more urgent struggle which we must needs prosecute with greater unity, earnestness, and hope than ever yet against ignorance and vice, the original sources whence want and every human woe issue forth? Is it not time to send forth fearless labourers and farseeing discoverers into the higher worlds of human intellect, which seem as though they were about to be forsaken, given up to the hordes of darkness and atheism, which are ready to seize upon them? Surely these are the points to which courage should be turned—the obstacles which our holy cohorts of the future must grapple with and overcome. These mighty impossibilities would become possible if all that vast mass of courage and strength, now swept away by the horrors of war, were to be transformed, as God would have it, and devoted to this holy work.

Have we not a right as Christians to hope, to ask

for these things now, so long after the Coming of
Jesus Christ, remembering that they were perceived
and foretold by the Prophets who went before Him?
Have we not a right to move all our brethren to that
self-devotion which alone can effect them; nay, more,
to that sacrifice which can win them? What means
Isaiah when he speaks of "them that shall renew
their strength" *(mutabunt fortitudinem)*; of those to
whom God in reward promises that "they shall mount
up with wings of eagles; they shall run and not be
weary, they shall walk and not faint?"[1] What does
the Prophet mean when he bids "the people renew
their strength?" *(gentes mutent fortitudinem.)*[2] He
means what he said before in announcing the Lord's
Coming, Who shall teach men to "beat their swords
into ploughshares, and their spears into pruning
hooks; nation shall not lift up sword against nation
neither shall they learn war any more."[3]

In all good faith, is it not time, after twenty centuries
of Christianity, that we understood these truths which
a Jewish Prophet proclaimed seven hundred years
before Christ? May we not well be ashamed of our
blindness, of our obstinacy in treading under foot all
reason, all religion? And we who are the weak and
scant soldiers of that new and sacred war, have we not
a tenfold right to call upon our brave, noble-hearted

[1] Isa. xl. 31.   [2] Isa. xli. 1.   [3] Isa. ii. 4.

brethren, soldiers of the old world, the old war; men more powerful than we ourselves, were they not slaves to a heathen god from Olympus, the bloodthirsty Mars, who now leads them to the slaughter by millions, crushing out the choicest of our human race too often on behalf of unrighteous, well-nigh always for a barren cause?

But I want to explain what I mean by the transformation of courage as displayed in Henri Perreyve.

V.

Truly Henri was the most courageous man I have ever met—courage was the most marked feature in his character. From his earliest childhood upwards, he always went straight at danger; always knew how to bear any pain without complaint. I never saw such a simple, straightforward resolution. This tone of mind may be traced in the following brief notes to me, which were the literal utterances of his heart under very serious illness :—

"MON BON PÈRE,—I am still ill, but so far without danger. I am content to expiate my faults, and our Lord gives me a true and important light. So all this will be good, whether for life or death."

And a few days later :—

"I am not very well, though not in any positive danger. Pray for me, and ask our Lord only to leave

me in this world if I can work in it for His Glory,
and for my own salvation."

But why was Henri lying there in much greater
danger than he says? Simply in consequence of an
act of courage, in fact one of downright temerity.

His first illness, which affected his whole life, was
unquestionably owing to exertions beyond his age and
strength. It was while he was working to excess,
reading law out of obedience to his father, and philosophy and theology to please himself, that the famous
Journées de Juin occurred; and in spite of his fragile
constitution and his barely seventeen years, nothing
could dissuade him from taking his gun and following
his father everywhere, doing real hard service by day
and by night for five days.

This mere boy wrote concerning these events as
follows :—

"Paris, July 7th, 1848.

[1] "MONSIEUR ET BIEN CHER AMI,—I received your
kind letter with no less gratitude than pleasure.
Just now, when everybody is seeking out friends and
relations in order to be sure of their safety, a letter
is a great proof of affection, and yours was met
with the welcome which any sign of remembrance
from those we love brings. As you are so good as

---

[1] M. Abbé German.

to be so anxious about me and my family, I must at once set your mind at ease. My father and I were out through all the days and nights of the struggle, without receiving the slightest wound, not certainly for lack of opportunity, for soldiers of the line and *gardes mobiles* fell continually beside us. The insurgents aimed specially at them, no doubt as being their most dangerous enemies. But our legion, too, counted up some deaths, about forty, among whom was M. le chef de bataillon Masson, an advocate, a man highly esteemed by every one. I will not repeat the story of our contests, which the newspapers have already told, but you may be satisfied that neither Saint Sulpice nor our own quarter has suffered. The struggle was concentrated in the Faubourg Saint Marceau, and it was there our legion was sent. I was not the only member of my college or class (Lycée Saint Louis, Rhétorique). There was great enthusiasm. I have been to inquire after M. Barch, who is well, though under arms all through the insurrection. I hear that he complains of not having received some honourable wound. Indeed, if one could but guide the ball oneself, a wound after such a combat would be precious ! You see that it is all good news as to ourselves, but alas ! Paris has suffered greatly in this terrible struggle. Last week we saw nothing but funeral processions, and yesterday there was a public ceremony in memory of the fallen. An immense altar on pillars, covered with silver draperies, with a veiled Cross, was raised in the Place de la Concorde, opposite the Allée des Champs Elysées. All the Corps de l'Etat assisted, regular regiments, legions of the *garde nationale* and the *garde mobile,* covered the great Place, and the very solemn stillness was only broken by the muffled drums and religious hymns sung by a numerous orchestra. The beautiful Place, the great avenue full of troops with their sparkling helmets, the Chambre des Députés and the Madeleine hung with black, and a brilliant sunshine,—the mixture of a dashing army and a funeral ceremony was altogether most striking. When the Host was elevated, and the mass of people knelt down, drums beating, choir chanting, and all the bells in the city pealing, it was a grand spectacle. One must confess that if our capital is horrible to behold on the day of battle, it is very beautiful, very fine on that of victory and triumph ! Forgive me, dear sir, for dwelling upon all these impressions ; you have always listened to all I have to say with so much kindness, that I look for the like indulgence now.

"To day Mgr. Affre, one of our greatest heroes, is buried, as well as Generals Négrier and de Bréa. How many acts of self-devotion, of courage, of self-

abnegation have risen out of our civil war! Is it
not God's intention to raise us out of our long sleep
by this terrible trial? If so, we may yet bless this
war, which, while it makes so many victims, may have
sent up a peace offering to Heaven, and rekindled
courage and grandeur in many a soul, amid the dying
and the dead. M. de Lamartine says in his 'Giron-
dins' that a nation need not deplore its blood when
shed to bring forth eternal truths!

"You see, *Monsieur et cher ami*, that I look upon our
epoch *en philosophe*, thereby anticipating somewhat
my next year's class. Anyhow, if I am not permitted
to enter upon philosophy this year, I shall always be
helped to rise above passing events, by that better
philosophy, *i.e.* religion, which, although less obscure
and abstract than the other, is not less rich in comfort
or fruitful in self-devotion. You were my first teacher
in that science, and, consequently, I can never think
of you without the most lively sense of gratitude, and
I hope you will allow me to add of friendship."

At this time Henri had joined a band of young
men, members of the Société de Saint Vincent de
Paul, who undertook to teach the poor children in
the Quartier Mouffetard. Their religious instruction
fell to his share; and, at last, all these exertions
brought on a violent spitting of blood, during which
his life was in great danger. The results of this

illness lasted during a year ; but he did not learn
prudence. Renewed overwork, fresh outbursts of
activity, brought on a similar attack and the like
danger when he was twenty-three. Once more his
natural strength brought him through, after a year's
struggle for life. The moment he was able, he set to
work again with all his usual energy, and, in 1857,
being then twenty-six, he was prepared to take the
important step towards the priesthood of receiving
deacon's orders. Accordingly, he entered the preparatory Retreat at Saint Sulpice ; and there, on the
second day of those exhausting spiritual exercises he
found himself once more attacked by that dreadful
congestion of the lungs—knowing full well that at
any moment death might come with one of those
violent attacks of hemorrhage. Nevertheless, Henri
said not a word, and followed all the Retreat for five
days, with death perpetually hanging over him. By
dint of intense energy he struggled on to the ordination day, and then, as he bowed himself down at the
solemn moment which dedicated him for ever, he was
forced to press a bloodstained handkerchief to his
lips, and to pass straight from the ordination into
the physician's hands, barely in time to be saved.
Another year of illness was the result : but he was a
deacon ! Henri told me of all this a few days later
in the following letter :—

" MY VERY EXCELLENT AND MOST DEAR FATHER,
—I must tell you something. On the second day
of my Retreat in the Séminaire de Saint Sulpice I got
congestion of the lungs. I said to myself, If I give
in before the ordination I shall not be a deacon, and
a deacon I must and will be. So I held out, and did
not give up the Retreat, but on Saturday last, after the
ordination, I was quite *à bout de forces.* I had only
just time to get to bed, and they bled me. To-day,
Wednesday, I can breathe rather better. One day,
during the Retreat, when I was very much upset, I
wrote four pages to you ; but, just as I was sending
my letter, I was seized with remorse, for I had complained in it ; so I tore it up !

"At last I am a deacon ! You will see that by
dint of perseverance, little by little, I shall attain to
the priesthood. *Introibo ad altare Dei.* In truth,
I hope some day to offer there a heart full of love to
God and man."

Yes, indeed, he attained his wish ; and on that day, [1]
the most eventful of his life, he asked these three
things :—

I. That he might be a humble priest ;

II. That he might never commit any mortal sin ;

III. That he might give his blood for Jesus Christ.

[1] He was ordained priest by Cardinal Morlot at Saint Sulpice,
May 29th, 1858.

This was the transformation of courage. His three great struggles with death had schooled him for warfare. And if you would know the results of his experience, the object at which thenceforth his transformed courage aimed, you will find them in those words which he calls, " *Retour à la Vie.*"

I quote what Henri wrote, as the exponent of what he was, because I know full well that he never said or wrote anything which he had not felt, resolved, or experienced. Such writers do exist, men whose souls are so full of faith, that they are truthful even in their details of style. Thus we may contemplate his own mind in that book of which he said himself, " 'That of which the author speaks has been experienced before it was written."

The Return to Life.

" My Son,—The gift of renewed life has not been given thee for thyself. This life which is restored, thou owest it to mankind for My Glory's Sake. And if, startled at so great a demand, thou wouldst evade it by asking to whom thou owest thy life, I answer, My son, that thou owest it to all men.

" A Christian belongs to all men, and he has a clear, unexceptional right to take part in the world's affairs. A Christian is a man who all through his life prays, ' Our Father, Thy kingdom come, Thy Will be done on earth as it is in Heaven.' What is that to say, My son, save that the Christian continually watches over the earth, and prays for it?

"The Apostle meant this when he said to the Christians of his time, 'I exhort, therefore, that first of all supplications, prayers, intercessions, and giving of thanks be made for all men;' as when, in the largeness of his all-embracing heart, he affirmed that none could be offended, or weak, or persecuted, without his sharing their affliction; and that he was consumed day by day by the care of all living souls.[1] This is what another Doctor of the Church meant when he boldly says, speaking of the priest, that 'he is placed as a sentinel over the whole world;' and going on to describe him as *chargé d'affaires* for all men, living and dead, has dared to say, 'The universe is a trust in his hands.'

"And this, My son, is true of every Christian. Death, whose approach thou hast felt, is often the voice which I use to bring home to My children the greatness of their vocation.

"The mere foreshadowing of death breaks through all narrowing bonds, and widens the circle of a man's thoughts, aspirations, and love. It gathers seasons together, does away with distance, brings the whole earth nearer, points out the fundamental relationship

[1] I. Tim. ii. 1.   II. Cor. xi.

F

which exists among all men. The exceeding simplicity of all things is suddenly set before him in a
vivid light : details vanish, all that must perish wanes,
and the soul remains alone with God and the world's
salvation before its eyes.

"Such, My son, is the sacred lesson of death.
Happy those souls who, having received it, return
to life to find it no mere barren remembrance."

Yet again, I call this the transformation of courage.
Death met face to face and understood : a life wholly
devoted to the welfare of mankind with a courage no
way inferior to that of the soldier, but more effectually
employed.

VI.

The minister of the Gospel has yet another and a
more difficult task to perform. It is not only courage
that has to be transfigured and transformed. Love must
be dealt with in like fashion. And here, you will say,
is the great difficulty of the sacerdotal sacrifice. Is it
right to sacrifice love, which is the very life of the
soul? Ought the heart of men to be left devoid of
affections ? My answer is that at no time, above all
in the present day, have men loved their own souls,
or God, or His invisible beauties, or that of their
brethren who are visible, or even that of the wife
God has given them, sufficiently. The great need is

to increase not to diminish love, and we say that it is increased by sacrifice.

But first of all, I would ask, what of that life of love in hearts that ignore sacrifice? Open your eyes, and study some of the most prominent features of the human race. Look upon the perverted idea of family life which prevails among the followers of Mahomet, who aim at faith through the sword, and seek to find a heaven in voluptuousness. What love do you find in his harem? What is the result of his plurality? Disgust and the overturn of all natural laws : the love of man for his lawful mate is destroyed by his dull ignorance of the law of sacrifice. Or do you imagine that fallen man, incapable as he is of loving even the material beauty which he beholds, will love the invisible beauty of justice and truth? Will he love honour, country, or the world's progress? Such a man knows naught of all such things, whether he be a follower of Mahomet or one of ourselves. All love is nullified where there is no sacrifice.

But on the other hand, all love has been reinstated on earth by the Gospel, and nothing can maintain it in our times save the Cross and the sacrifice of the Cross. The evangelic sacrament of love, a necessary accompaniment of sacrifice, maintains family love. Sacerdotal sacrifice, in its wholesale character, brings forth all love, visible and invisible.

It teaches men to love their visible brother and sister with a mighty love, strong even as death; and no less to love the invisible beauty of the things of God.

This was the mind of Henri Perreyve. He saw, he carried out all this. As he transformed the mighty courage with which God had gifted him, even so he transformed the immense powers of love which filled his heart. I know that heart's history; I know the magnitude of its sacrifice. But I know too the new heart which God gave him, and therein I saw the full meaning of those words, "the transfiguration of love," which he uses in writing the life of Rosa Ferrucci. "It is the glory of Christianity," he says, after describing the death of that bright, gifted betrothed bride, "to have made a reality of that holy love of which ancient philosophy dreamed, but which it had never known or beheld. It is the glory of Christ's religion to have so taught and trained man's heart as to make it thus simultaneously pure and powerful; more and more capable of loving with an ever strengthening love all that is loveable on earth, while yet capable of loving it all less than God! It is the glory of Christ's religion to have taught a mere child, not a philosopher or a poet, but a simple pious maiden, well nigh unconsciously to realize the sublimest heights of human wisdom, the perpetual tendency of all love, of all earthly shadows

of being and beauty, to flow back to their source—
Infinite Beauty Itself; the inevitable return of all
' divine phantoms,' as Plato calls them, to eternal
reality. It is the glory of Christianity that it has on
all sides opened the way for man to approach God,
teaching him to use all his affections, as so many
steps whereby to ascend to absolute love. ' Ascen-
siones in corde suo disposuit.' [1] And finally it is the
glory of Christ's religion to have worked this wonder,
—namely that the most exalted saintliness, the most
superhuman perfection do not in any way destroy or
hinder our pure earthly affections—so that Saints do
not learn to love God above all things through lack
of love to others, but rather by loving all the world
better than themselves, and God better than all the
world !

" If, following out this thought, you will ponder
upon the inner nature and history of our heart when
left to itself, you will be forced to admit that it under
goes a very transfiguration.

" And in death this transfiguration is, if possible,
more striking still. Death has learnt from the Cross
that its final task is to be the auxiliary of love : an
indissoluble brotherhood was formed there between
these two mighty powers, and love received the

[1] English version, " In whose heart are Thy ways." Ps.
lxxxiv. 5.

mission to transform death into a sacrifice. And therefore it is that we do not find our ideal of the dying Christian in the old statue of the Dying Gladiator—who dies resigned, but passive, his head sunken, his dimmed eye fixed upon this earth which is passing rapidly from his grasp, his heart perturbed at the vague darkness and uncertainty before him. No, our ideal is the Crucified Son of Man, upright, raised above the earth, '*exaltatus a terra,*' in the attitude of a priest at the altar. His eyes raised to His Father in heaven, forgiving man, loving him to the end, consenting to die, Himself willing it. solemnly commending His Soul into the Hands of God —at once subject to and King of death, at once Victim and Pontiff. This is indeed the Christian brother-hood of love and death."[1]

It was thus Henri spoke in one of his earliest writings,[2] and on the last occasion that his voice was heard in public (preaching in the Church of the Sorbonne, on the festival of Corpus Christi, May, 1864, the *Fête de l'Amour*, as he called it), he dwelt at length on the true characteristics of holy love.

"There are two great laws in love," he said ; "laws to which God has ever vouchsafed to subject Himself : I would define them as the law of progress, and the

---

[1] Biographies et Panégyriques, p. 215.
[2] His sketch of Rose Ferrucci was written in 1858.

final law.[1] It is a primary law in love that it cannot
exist without growth. It must increase, it must be
ever rising, it must gain fresh strength alike from
gladness and from woe, it must grow deeper through
happiness, deeper still through trial and sacrifice ; in
a word, it must be continually moving, it must ever
go onwards. And here a single glance is enough to
tell why love is so scant upon earth. What created
being is worthy to be the aim of such progress? What
mortal treasure can win this ever kindling affection ?
God Alone can satisfy such vastness of desire without
satiety or exhaustion. And, therefore, Christianity
has done a Godlike work in making God the necessary medium between those who love one another.
Christianity fathoms man's heart : it knows well that
every really deep love has a secret yearning after that
which is infinite, and that if this yearning is the rock
whereon profane earthly passion splits, it is the very
strength and health of all holy love, inasmuch as it
alone can uphold and sustain love by opening the
way to endless growth. Oh my God, in that Thou
givest Thyself to Thy children, Thou hast assured that
to them which the world without Thee can never give,
an Everlasting Love ! Thou hast taught them to look
beyond self ; thou hast given them an inexhaustible

[1] " La loi de la marche et la loi du terme." Station de la
Sorbonne. " L'amour de Dieu et des hommes," p. 208.

stream wherein to slake their thirst; Thou hast sheltered
them from those earthly gulfs wherein our fleeting
earthly joys perish, while yet proclaiming themselves eternal . . . .

"I have called the second law of love the final law,
because there comes a time when, having exhausted
all its gifts, love has but one thing left to give—
ITSELF. The moment comes when, having given intellect, fortune, time, thought, the past and the future,
he who loves can take but one step more, and give
himself for ever,—never to recall the gift; body and
soul, mind and being given to Him Who first gave the
gift of love. And this law of love is written by God's
Own Hand in His Gospel, where the Holy Spirit records of the Son of God that 'having loved His own,
He loved them unto the end,'—*in finem dilexit eos.* It
was then, after He had given Himself wholly, after He
had called them His friends, and told them all that
was to come, He gave them His very Body as a pledge
for ever. Surely this was the end, the very final abyss
of love! and to this He loved us,—*in finem dilexit.*

"Oh God, grant us such an ever kindling love as
may make us worthier Thee as life goes on, our hearts
more like to Thine. Give us that final love, so that
we may give ourselves to Thee.

". . My friends, do you love God? It is a startling,
a terrible question, but it is one we all greatly need

to ask ourselves within the silent depths of our own heart . . . .

" The day will come when all that you have done for God will seem utterly insufficient, and when, over-powered by the blessed longing to do more, you will seek to give yourself to Him for ever. What shape will this offering take ? I know not. There are well nigh as many several ways of making it as there are several souls in this great assembly. The religious life is very far from being the only form in which it can be made. The magistrate may give himself wholly to God without quitting his office ; the soldier need not lay down his sword, or the artist his pencil ; it is an unseen offering, made within the heart's most secret depth, and many a time the truest sacrifice is altogether unknown to those around . . . .

" But blessed, thrice blessed, those virgin hearts whom God takes in their first freshness of life for His special service, and who, as they go onwards early find that sacred term of total self-abnegation. Happy their lot, those brides of Christ, who from the first have lavished all that tender self-devotion, all that hidden world of passionate love upon Christ, which they will never lavish on earthly things ! And you, my young brethren and friends, if amid your youthful ardour, if in the very midst of your pride of liberty, Jesus Christ should call to you with the same everlasting words which drew the Apostles to His Side, 'Come, follow Me;' count it indeed as a mighty honour, bow your head beneath the weight of glory, and trembling though loving, accept the sacerdotal crown, which like that of Jesus, is studded with thorns, but which leaves its marks of blood upon our brow for the love of man and for the Glory of God. . . . .

"Let us beware of being mere humanitarians, who losing sight of the soul, aim at naught save material progress. The inefficiency of all such blind bene-factors of mankind is too notorious to need demon-stration. But, on the other hand, let us beware of that subtle refinement which affects to ignore all save that which is spiritual, and which disdains to care for the physical sufferings of our brethren. Such was not the mind of Christ. 'Non ita didi-cistis Christum.'[1] Wheresoever Jesus met with human suffering He paused to give it a heedful pity. When the sick were brought to Him His Gracious Hands were at once stretched out to bless; the sorrowful cry of a beggar by the wayside drew Him forthwith to impart healing both of body and soul; His Divine Hand designed to touch the leper's wounds; He wept beside the grave of Lazarus; He sorrowed with the widow over her son, with the Centurion over his little daughter. Do not aim at being more loosed from

---

[1] Eph. v. 20.

earthly ties, more spiritual than the Son of God; let us know how to weep over the sufferings of mankind.

" . . . . It is with this suffering body that we have to deal. This body is the most sacred of all God's material works; this flesh was taken upon Him by Jesus Christ; dwelt in by His life, purified by His purity, transfigured with Him on Mount Tabor, consecrated for ever, the Sacrifice above all others, upon the Cross. We should deal reverentially with it; we may not despise any particle of its poverty; we must not turn a deaf ear to any of its groans. . . . In this day it seems to me that no intelligent independent Christian man should suffer himself to be outstripped in the study and practical application of the social sciences. The Christian should not tolerate that the world be better able to deal than ourselves with those great questions which are so powerfully, so inevitably at work amongst us, questions which the Gospel alone has called forth; I mean such as pauperism, labour, family ties, association, mutual aid, refuges and asylums, the labour of women and children—questions of the most vital importance, and which concern the most essential foundations of human society. I would that we were leaders in every attempt at social amelioration; I would that by reason of our Christianity we were above all other men alive to every

such movement. A Christian is a man to whom
Jesus Christ intrusts all his fellow men; nothing can
be foreign to him which concerns any one of his
brethren. There should not be a single discovery, a
new organization or association for good, no effort to
soothe suffering, no enterprise, no invention to lighten
human toil, but we ought to be the first to know, to
examine, to develop, to devote time, money, energy,
hope, life itself to the object ; this is most assuredly
our duty. There is a twofold race of men upon the
earth—the one that harms souls, the other that works
for their good. Both exercise a great power in the
world. They are for ever sundered far apart, striving
one against the other ; they are as utterly opposed to
one another as God is to evil. The one boldly and
insolently sows broadcast impurity, falsehood, violence,
treachery, dishonour, bitter tears, despair, and finds
pleasure in so doing. The other bears with it reverence, love, light, the joy of a pure heart, immortal
affection, honour, courage as to this world, hope as to
that which is to come ; and this class of men also
find delight in so doing. . . . .

"My brethren, it is a goodly thing to die with the
happy consciousness of never having been any
hindrance to the soul of another ; to die knowing
that one has not offended any of God's little ones, of
whom our Lord says that their Angels behold the Face

of our Father Which is in Heaven. To die with the
blessed consciousness of never having taken advantage
of another's infirmity, or poverty, or ignorance, never
to have dealt with the sacred weakness of God's
feebler creation, save to respect, defend, protect her;
to die able to say that one has not extended the
empire of evil upon the earth by one hair's breadth;
but that upon the other hand, one has enlarged the
sacred borders of that which is good; that one has
expended mind, years, fortune and strength on behalf
of the kingdom of truth and justice. Surely this is
a true consolation, a real stay amid the closing
shadows of coming death—a true claim to man's
respect, to God's protection!"

Yet a brief while and Henri Perreyve himself fulfilled these words. It was truly thus that he died,
with even such a sacred joy at his heart.

Bear with me, if I return to the point from which I
started, and seek yet further to define this transformation and transfiguration of love. It is a sacrifice of
love, whereby that love is increased on earth. Just
as the converse, *i.e.*, the absence of self-sacrifice in an
individual, an age, or a nation annihilates love (and
this is a universal historical fact), so self-sacrifice,
indispensable not to priests alone, but in some shape
to every Christian and every man, leads the soul
from death to life. It does not substitute or abstract

Platonic love of mankind for that which is personal
and concrete. It creates a real, substantial, individual
love, which is the life, the blessing, the essential
strength of the world. It leads us from death to life,
from darkness to life, into the new heart of Christianity.
Thereby we perceive that when Christ and His
Apostles spoke of love, they were using no mere form
of words, but rather were opening a new world to us :
we learn to understand what Jesus meant when He
said, "I lay down My life for My friends;" or
S. John, "We know that we have passed from death
unto life, because we love the brethren. He that
loveth not his brethren abideth in death." The soul
thus united to God and its brethren tastes true happiness ; it loves no visionary abstraction, but a human
reality, a Living God. Without such love nothing can
make us happy; with it, nothing can deprive us of
happiness. A man's life is given through such love
to men ; his world of compassion covers all suffering;
his one ideal of life is to save and lead to the light all
those who lie in darkness and the shadow of death,
while yet they have the elements of goodness and
happiness in them.

This is the priest's work; this is his holy vocation.
Jesus, Our Great High Priest, asked, "Lovest thou
Me?" "Thou knowest, Lord, that I love Thee"—
and the consequence, the proof was to be, "Feed My

sheep;" be a fisher of men, that thou mayest lead them all to love, to glory, and to eternal happiness.

This is Christ's call to His labourers, and this is the key to Henri Perreyve's intense desire to receive his priestly commission, when, after years of ill health, it seemed as though God were about to call him hence before that grace was given him. It was under this keen impression that he wrote the following words to his friend Charles Perraud, who was about to be ordained priest before him :—

Hyères, Dec. 1857.

. . . . "I want to tell you, dearest Charles, that this very morning, in spite of all my longing desire to attain to the priesthood, a yet stronger feeling has taken possession of my soul. I feel that I could even sacrifice that joy of joys, that sole object of my life,[1] to the Will of my Master, and that I could accept death before I take my place at His Altar, although to die thus would be a tenfold sacrifice, a tenfold bitterness of death !"

[1] Cette raison unique de toute ma vie."

CHAPTER III.

ORGANIZATION OF LIFE.

I.

IT was thus that from his very childhood God's Grace and the energy of his own overflowing heart led Henri Perreyve to seek the true perfection of life, *i.e.* the consecration of life to labour and sacrifice out of love to God and man. And from the first, he selected the highest form of such consecration—the Christian Priesthood.

And even therein he aimed at what is best and highest. As there are various grades in our armies, so is there abundant diversity of work in the Church's army. "There are diversities of gifts," S. Paul says; "*divisiones operationum sunt.*" And, he goes on, "Covet earnestly the best gifts . . . but rather that ye may prophesy." "*Æmulamini autem meliora charismata . . . . magis autem ut prophetetis.*"[1]

What does the Apostle mean by prophecy? He tells us, the power of "speaking unto men to edifica-

---

[1] I. Cor. xii. 4, 31 ; xiv. 1.

tion, and exhortation, and comfort."[1] "*Nam qui prophetat hominibus loquitur ad ædificationem, exhortationem, consolationem.*"

This precept Henri obeyed. Of all spiritual gifts and ministerial offices he mainly "coveted" that of prophecy; from childhood his ambition was to bear the words of exhortation and consolation to his fellow men. When eighteen he had clearly decided that the Lord's Mission, "*Ecce Ego mitto ad vos prophetas et sapientes et scribas,*" was committed to him, and he accepted the charge of speaking, writing, teaching, enlightening, comforting the flock of Christ.

It was a mighty ambition for a mere boy; how was he to make ready for such a work? Not, most assuredly in the spirit of those "scribes" who set forth rather in pride than love; who attempt to wield the sacred Ministry of the Word without being called thereto, without due preparation; whose undisciplined, unthoughtful minds are influenced mainly by impulse or chance. Every man who truly aims at serving his country and his race must toil; the engineer, the lawyer, the soldier, the sailor, all are prepared to give themselves up to years of hard study; how much more must they do so who aim to fulfil the sacred task of teaching and guiding and comforting mankind in God's Own Name! Israel had their "company of prophets,"[2]

---

[1] I Cor. xiv. 3   [2] I Sam. xix. 20.

and the Church has ever had her company, her schools of prophets, missionaries, martyrs, doctors, authors. These schools we call "seminaries," because therein are cultivated the seeds of wisdom and knowledge which God vouchsafes to plant among those called to be His husbandmen. And Henri prepared to submit himself to five years' training in philosophy and theology, under the strict discipline of obedience, rule, and recollection. But, here again, his eager search after an ideal perfection led him to join one of the noblest undertakings of the Christian mind, an undertaking the success of which I believe will be a blessing to the world.

For three centuries the Church, following the line started by the Council of Trent under the guidance of S. Philip Neri, S. Carlo Borromeo, S. Vincent de Paul, and others, has laboured at two ends :—I., the organization of schools for training candidates for the Priesthood; and II., the organization of the priest's own life. The first object is by degrees being effectually carried out throughout the Catholic world. We may venture to speak of the priest's education as organized. But the daily life of the secular priest is not so, and its great deficiency may be briefly summed up—he is too much alone.

No doubt the missionary, whose fellow-labourer is cut off by death, may be called upon to remain alone with his crucifix; the country curate (that other missionary!) may remain for years alone in his desert of ignorance and indifference. But would it not be possible greatly to lessen the perilous isolation of many among Christ's soldiers? Christ sent forth His Apostles two and two; "*misit binos ante faciem suam*"—and we know why: "Where less than two are love cannot exist."[1] Cardinal de Bérulle says that a community life is almost essential to the clergy;[2] and surely to them, above all others, the inspired words apply: "Behold, how good and joyful a thing it is for brethren to dwell in unity."

Therefore it is that so many eminent saints and servants of God have striven to lessen the isolation of the secular priest. Without converting him into a monk, they have aimed at the institution of communities in which union and freedom, individual action and community life, should be combined. This was Bossuet's ideal when he spoke of a sacerdotal society which should have no mind save that of the Church, no rules save her canons, no superiors save her bishops, no bond save charity, no vows save those of baptism and holy orders.[3]

[1] "Quia minus quam inter duos charitas haberi non potest."

[2] "La vie commune et sociale est presque essentielle à l'état ecclésiastique."

[3] "Ce dessein de société sacerdotale, qui ne doit avoir d'autre esprit que l'esprit de l'Eglise, ni d'autres règles que ses canons,

No one felt all this more fully than Cardinal de
Bérulle, who, when founding the "Oratoire de France,"
took pains to declare that he was not seeking to
found a new Order, but simply to promote the Order
of Priests : an order which, he said, was founded by
no saint, but by our Lord Jesus Christ Himself, Who
is its Everlasting Superior ; a mighty order, whose
visible heads are the Vicar of Christ and his Bishops ;
an order which may be assisted by a more perfect though
wholly free organization, such as Cardinal de Bérulle
sought to realize in the congregation of the Oratory.

This realization we find in the Oratory of S. Philip
Neri.[1] A few priests grouped together, united in
community life, but without vows ; independent in
their work, but helping, strengthening, cheering one
another, subject to no rule save that of the Church
generally, and their own Bishop specifically. Neither
superior, general, nor central house—independence in
every house, as in ordinary families. Would not such
organization, more generally spread, tend infinitely to

ni d'autres Supérieurs que ses Evêques, ni d'autre lien que la
charité, ni d'autres vœux que ceux du sacerdoce et du baptême."—
Oraison funèbre du Père Bourgoing.

[1] S. Philip Neri founded the Congregation of the Priests of
the Oratory at Rome. The congregation grew out of an association of priests which he joined immediately after his ordination in 1551, and it was formally authorized by a bull of Pope
Gregory XIII., in 1575.

the strengthening of the Priesthood? If all priests were thus united, either as resident members, or as scattered members who might yet have a link to the centres of work, prayer, and study called "Oratories," would they not double their usefulness?

As to the Oratoire de France, of which I am a member, far be it from me to depreciate it because of its centralized government. S. Francis de Sales said of the Cardinal de Bérulle, that he would gladly quit his diocese to live under that great man's guidance, inasmuch as nothing could be holier or more serviceable to God's Church than his congregation. The Oratoire is a brotherly association of secular priests, bound by no vows, all authority vested in the congregation itself, its superiors our Bishops, its constitutions amenable to a general assembly.

Surely were such centres of intellectual and moral association more numerous, under the blessing of God's Holy Spirit they would do much towards the advancement of the priestly calling. How many brave men, crushed and saddened by their isolated positions, would find fresh strength in such a *point d'appui* for their toil! Might not such associations furnish strength, and mutual kindling of love to God and man, for the effecting of those mighty enterprizes of zeal, love, and science of which we stand so sorely in need? Think what an enormous power is wielded by industrial association! How much more might intellectual association for moral and religious work effect! Would not such united efforts have power to overstep the moral and religious hindrances which sever the East, Africa, and Asia from our western centres of civilization? and might we not thereby look to see that harmony of the intellectual and religious world established for which we all so greatly yearn? Might not peace be restored thereby to the human mind, peace to the nations of the world?

On all sides we find the workmen of Europe struggling to organize a free association among themselves, and when the day comes that God's labourers do the like, we shall see among them those great works of which S. Bernard prophesied:—" *firmissima vi rectitudinis consistent.*"

It was under the influence of some such thoughts and hopes, more or less clearly defined, that Henri Perreyve was led, by the Grace of God, to that spot where he found the two things he sought—a school of priestly discipline, and therein, amid brotherly union, a real organization of life.

II.

It was at this time that Henri's dear friend Charles Perraud told him of his calling to the Priesthood, and the two prepared to set forth together; " misit binos ante faciem suam." But Charles Perraud had a brother, one of that group of youths, all pupils of the École Normale, who about this year of excitement, 1848, had resolved to devote themselves enthusiastically to the welfare of mankind. These young men proposed to live together, and work together according to the various faculties God had given them, to promote the triumph of the Christian faith, the one true source of all peace, knowledge, order, justice, and freedom.

This little group was the seed whence was to spring a tree planted by our Heavenly Father; destined to thrive and bear much fruit. Henri Perreyve was led to join them by his friend Charles Perraud, and soon after, by a happy coincidence of providential circumstances, they forcibly took possession—not without some difficulty—of a holy priest who undertook their guidance,[1] and thus began the restoration of the Oratoire de France.

Henri Perreyve has recorded in an MS. called " Souvenirs intimes sur Frédéric Ozanam," how he first confided his intentions to that beloved master. " About this time," he says, "I left Eaux Bonnes,

---

[1] The R. P. Pététot. The new Oratory was revived in Aug. 1852, at the Presbytère de Saint Roch, six members forming the nucleus.—" L'Oratoire de France," p. 377, par le P. Adolphe Perraud.

and went for a little tour in Spain. Just before going
I dined with M. Ozanam, and in the evening as we
sat over the fire, talking very confidentially, I felt that
the time was come to tell my great secret to my
revered friend. I did it simply and easily, feeling
half ashamed and half triumphant. What, I said to
myself, will he think of me, knowing as he does how
thoughtless, how fond of amusement, how childish in
the worst sense I am ? will he forgive me for trying to
combine so weighty a resolution with such frivolous
tastes ? But somehow I took courage, and having
once broken the ice, it became quite natural to me to
pour my heart into his.

"That evening I more thoroughly understood M.
Ozanam than ever before. It was with tears of affection, of fatherly kindness, and of holy earnestness and
enthusiasm that he answered me. Our wish to
devote ourselves to God's Service by means of science
and literature, our plan of joining the Abbé Gratry,
then Chaplain of the École Normale, and our dream
of a studious congregation which we did not as yet
call the *Oratoire ;*—all these dreams and hopes, which
might never come to anything, assumed a living
reality at once to a soul so ready to believe in all
that is good, as his was. He looked at it all, not
as we then were, or as we are actually, or even
as we can hope to be for a long time ; and if

anything can be a consolation for not having had him
to assist in these humble beginnings of our work
which have been so blessed by God, it is the knowledge that at all events our first start was appreciated
by him. All through that evening he cheered me with
his kindly words and good wishes, and then with a
close embrace, we parted.

" I went homewards, intoxicated with joy, hope and
strength. I wanted to feed upon my happiness in
solitude, far from all men. It was late—but un-
heeding that, I took a mountain path, and went on
like a madman, looking at the heavens, regardless of
earth. Suddenly an instinct made me draw hastily
back; I was on the very edge of a precipice; one
step more, and I must have fallen; I took fright, and
gave up my nocturnal wanderings."

Dearly beloved child, you need not fear; you were
upheld by angels. I believe in the loving promise,
" They shall bear thee in their hands, that thou hurt
not thy foot against a stone." The angels bore
you up all your life, until they bore you to God's
Bosom.

Your bright dreams were not unreal, any more than
the enthusiasm of our dear Ozanam. Let us be content to wait. After your death, my son, after mine,
the seed which we call the *Oratoire* will bear fruit,
when in His own good time the Holy Spirit sheds

His light upon its now frail, quivering spark of science
and intellect. Meanwhile the day came when the
little band of friends took possession of their promised
land, a humble dwelling capable of holding only
seven persons. But the dream was realized; the
friends who met there were about to live together,
pray together, and work together. There ensued some
few bright years of real happiness, of close brotherly
friendship, saintly life, and real fruitful work, both
intellectual and spiritual. Beneath that austere
though gentle rule, and under a holy and humble
example, were moulded some true priestly souls,
good and patient, humble, loving, brave. The friends
set to work with zealous delight upon the special
studies to which a priest is bound—philosophy and
theology—and several began for the first time to
experience the advantages and the difficulties of real
intellectual association.

That truly was a golden age, and dear Henri Perreyve was its brightest sunbeam! How shall I describe
the overflowing cheerfulness and fun, of which he was
always the life, or the earnest religious conversations in
which not unfrequently tears were shed, and which
ended by our falling on our knees in thankfulness to
God? Sometimes, after there had been some more than
usually touching instruction on Gospel words given in
the chapel, Henri would be so full of gratitude that,

unable to express it speedily enough *vivâ voce*, he
would write such notes as the following, which is a
fair illustration of the interior and mind of that little
group of men, the first fruits of the *Oratoire*—" One
can't keep from telling you, *bon et cher Père*, how happy
one was made by your homily this morning, and long
afterwards ; indeed, how happy one still is, all because
of it. You must know, too, that while you are
preaching there is a soul, a very poor and weakly
one, which quivers with appreciation, which gives
itself to God, which calls for His Blessing upon you,
which vibrates thus between our Lord and you, and
finds no rest save in saying from the very depths of
the heart, ' Dear Lord Jesus, it is Thou that speakest
to me in the words of our good Father : Thou knowest
how my heart accepts and yearns after the noble
thoughts which he sets before us. Help me to carry
them out fully ; do with me what Thou wilt, so that I
may serve our dearly loved brethren, that I may do
good to men, that I may help to lead them from their
false standard.' The soul of which I speak often says
such things, but after hearing you, it says them with
such love, such tears, and such hope, that the furrow
deepens, and that soul is quite filled with enthusiastic
energy for some hours ! Do you forgive me, father,
for saying all this ? What shall I say ? . . . I did
not know how to deal with the happiness you roused

in me this morning : it overwhelms me ; I want to
do something, and I can do nothing and am fit for
nothing. There is an almost grotesque disproportion
between what I long for and what I am ; and hence
springs a sort of *malaise*, an inward commotion which
would fain do great things. It is a sensation I have
often experienced ; all beautiful things are sure to
produce it in me—very beautiful music, very precious
friendship, a very striking sermon. How often I have
come away from Notre Dame with it, during Père
Lacordaire's reign ! Well, I had not felt it for long,
but you have revived it in me, and I want to thank
you for it, and that is why I write. I have found it
out now, but I really did not know when I began
my note !

"All this, *mon bon Père*, is to tell you that one loves
you, one prays for you, one rejoices to be your child.
your pupil ; one would fain be a stranger who would
have a right to pay you compliments, only one would
much rather belong to you, and promise most heartily
to give oneself up to our Dear Lord. So now I will
leave you in peace, not without feeling somewhat
ashamed of all this, which I don't altogether understand myself, but which I think God understands
better than we do, and will accept. Yours most
respectfully in our Lord."

"Filioli, diligite alteratrum !" " Little children, love

one another." Surely the Apostle of love was himself breathing this precept into our hearts from Heaven itself.

The minds of our little band felt their position favourable to combined study of true philosophy, both theoretical and practical, as also to that of theology in heart and mind. We really carried out that after which a large-hearted philosopher [1] sighed, when in his sorrowful speculations he taught that "philosophy concerns the soul, even as poetry and religion. Poetical, religious, and philosophical souls are sisters, inasmuch as poetry, religion, and philosophy are but several manifestations of a like sentiment."

We really carried this out in our school of philosophy. One saw and felt, in one's own very life, that poetry, religion, and philosophy are but manifestations of one and the same life. One realized that true prayer and hearty practical morality are the source of light and philosophy; one realized that a poetical warmth of soul is as necessary to science as experience and observation; that truly, "philosophy is a thing of the soul, like poetry and religion, and that he who seeks it with his mind only may become a philosopher some day, but he has proved that he is not such yet." [2]

---

[1] Jouffroi. Mélanges philosophiques, 2e édit. I. 417.
[2] *Ibid.*

These followers of light, to finding which they wholly devoted themselves, carried out their philosophic researches in spirit and in truth. But before all else, they perceived that they were and must ever be as mere children when brought face to face with boundless sight and infinite knowledge. Such is the wise and inevitable humility which true philosophy should teach, thereby preparing the way for theology—that is to say, for a respectful meditation upon God's revealed truths, which are greater far than our minds ; truths the substance of which is in us through faith, while their mystery cannot be fathomed by our intelligence.

III.

The chief point on which I would dwell here, however, is the experience we gained as to the reality, the necessity, and the difficulties of intellectual association.

Men have but little community of thought ; this is a melancholy practical truth. They combine the results of their mental efforts when made, and that is something, as the last three centuries have shown, towards the extension of physical and natural science. But, at the first start, seeking and finding, each mind works alone. Now would not combined action multiply the vigour of mental effort and its results ?

I have often thought that a band of five or six men.

living together, loving one another, working together for a like object, striving to carry out the Apostolic words, "erant omnes unanimiter in eodem loco," would constitute an intellectual power such as we have not yet known. So far as my brief experience goes, the result is an intellectual stream which bears one forcibly onwards : each individual moves, but the road on which we travel also moves with us. It is not a sixfold power only, it is the power of all those combinations which may be produced by six unities, of which each is a living power.

These are facts, which it seems to me time that we should understand, and I unhesitatingly reaffirm what was said in connection with analogous studies by a physiologist [1] some quarter of a century since, " that it is time for science to give heed to phenomena which are so numerous and so well established, however strange." I mean the direct spiritual communication which exists between souls ; an order of facts as common as marvellous, which the rude carelessness of false science and the trivialities of life succeed in forcing men to disregard.

For my own part, absolute experience constrains me to say that not only spiritual movement but also intellectual movement is, in certain cases, directly transmissible from one soul to another, and that

[1] Burdach.

without any intervention of tripods or turning tables !
Such influences affect us all daily, only people do not
heed them. I speak of what I have seen and felt
myself, and when the day comes that science explores
this vast and fertile region, men will marvel that they
have so long had eyes and yet saw not.

Some time since, Friedrich Fichte spoke happily
on the subject in his " Psychologia ; " Burdach, as I
have already said, affirms the fact as experimentally
certain ; Laplace treats of it in a little-known work. I
admit his facts, without accepting his hypothesis. I
prefer that of Fénelon when he says, " It is in this
centre that men from all the ends of the world meet
together." " What," cries out ignorance, conven-
tionalism, and practical materialism, " minds and
souls meet in God !" But of a truth in that home
where we were gathered so closely together in heart,
thoughts, and hope, how often one was positively
invaded by conditions of mind emanating from
another ; pursued by heart stirrings and thoughts
which were the offspring of another brain ! I hardly
dare repeat details which seem too strange to be
true :—*e.g.*, "Who is it, that since last evening, all night,
and this morning, has persisted in investigating this
notion, which had not been started yesterday ? I
fancy that it is you!" " Yes, it is I," Henri Perreyve
immediately answered.

But we will not go farther into this psychological analysis; we will keep to what is obvious to every one, and that is, that in such an association of minds each man acquires fresh power, and greater wisdom in using it. Thus upheld and encouraged by one another, full of hope and trust, we looked forward to some day realizing that intellectual union, through which, "omnes unanimiter in eodem loco," we might undertake a real Encyclopædia.[1] As we know, S. Philip Neri had already proposed such an aim : the Père Thomassin, single-handed, attempted a sort of Christian Encyclopædia, in a course of works called " L'Art d'Enseigner Chrétiennement," treating the writings of heathen philosophers, historians, and poets, as well as the natural sciences. We were keenly alive to what has since become yet more obvious, namely, the way in which every literary channel has been invaded by the spirit of infidelity, negation, and abhorrence of Christianity. "The enemy seizes everything as a ground of attack," we said; "let us equally seize everything on the defensive side." Men fancy they have found a witness against Christianity in every isolated detail of science; let us meet such discordant straggling efforts by a united effort, by the unanimous witness of comparative science ; let us demonstrate

[1] See " Discours sur les devoirs intellectuels des prêtres de l'Oratoire."

the harmony that really exists between it and the Gospel, in a real Encyclopædia.

We yet hope to realize such a work, and by a combination of men and of strength to fulfil that which Joseph de Maistre foretold in the beginning of this century.

"Look out," he said, "for the coming man of science, who, strong in the natural affinity of science and religion, will combine the two with a marvellous light, which will put an end to the evil period of incredulity now warping the human mind."

Our ambition was to establish a focus of permanent work, of intellectual labour, a league of workmen, of real thinkers, whose mental powers would be combined, and who would help to demonstrate the real harmony of science and religion ; who would, in short, promote that work of God which a great Bishop has described France as feeling after for well nigh a century, though hitherto unable to obtain.

Such were our hopes, and such they are yet, as wide, but more enlightened.

In the first stage of any undertaking we for the most part feel boundless hope ; but the second, which brings us face to face with difficulties, too often savours of despair. Let us learn how to bear with this, and reach the third stage, namely, difficulties conquered, and the triumph of our ideal. Let us take courage ; a clear sight of our difficulties is the

first step towards triumph. They who set forth without presumption, expecting weighty hindrances, learn
by experience what the obstacle and difficulties really
are. And in this matter of a philosophical and
scientific apostolate our two difficulties are the difficulty of recollection and the necessity of daily
external work. A true encyclopædia, the demonstra-
tion of the harmony between science and religion,
cannot be attained by a juxtaposition of scientific
detail. On the contrary, it is precisely these very
sciences and details which need to be penetrated by
some few broad, deep, simple ideas, capable of
melting them as in a furnace, till they are transfigured
with light, even as crystallization transfigures carbon
into diamonds. But such a work requires to be done
not by minds which grovel in the dust of mere facts;
it requires rather a spirit recollected in God, capable
of intention and of contemplation, before anything
can be accomplished.

It is always harder than we are apt to suppose for
human nature to attain that deep recollection within
substantial truth, within the central source of light,
within that depth whither calm peace and blessed certainty so powerfully draw the soul. But in these
disturbed times, when all is struggle and confusion,
when the daily press keeps up an endless excitement
when every wind of the intellectual atmosphere is let

loose, it is harder than ever to dwell in that sanctuary
where recollection and words of truth abide.   Every
one wants to act, to speak, to fight.   No one is
willing to abide in his own room, as Pascal would
have us do.   No one is willing to obey the Gospel
precept, and shut his door, " clauso ostio," in order
to seek light in the most hidden recollection.   Who
believes in the real Presence of God, in the necessity
and possibility of beholding and interrogating It as a
means of knowing the truth ?   As a venerable Archbishop lately said to me, " Who in these days cares
for all that, *mon ami ?*   Who makes any attempt to
rise beyond that hopeless surface life which satisfies
the greater number of minds ? "

This is our interior difficulty.   But there is another
no less to be feared because exterior, the rather that
it often is the source of the first ; I mean the necessity of daily external work that men may earn their
daily bread.

Intuition and contemplation are not visible labour.
The far off preparation which is to lead to that stu-
pendous work of comparative science is a seed
destined to bear no visible fruit until many toilsome
years have passed.   The attempt to reduce science
into harmony with eternal philosophy, with the
eternal, essential, universal religion of the human
race, is one of those great works which is doomed to

many a failure in its first attempts. It is an undertaking, as I said, which God has vainly required of
man during the last century. One could name
several bands of priests in France who in our own
day have combined to attempt it. But after some
few years of struggle against hunger, they have all
been forced to become professors or tutors, in order
to have wherewithal to live.

If the old *Oratoire de France* had but lasted, if a
century's interval had not occurred, if its houses, its
libraries, its colleges, its traditions had but remained,
the work of blending science with the light of Christian truth would now amaze the world by its might
and splendour. Philosophy and general science
would not be as they now are, and the mocking
sophists who harass those who are incapable of self
defence would not be where they are. The strong
craftsmen of real philosophy and of science raised to
God's service would have taught the world the intellectual truth of Pascal's saying, "Religion must be so
entirely the centre that all must end there." They
would have continued and developed Thomassin
splendidly ; they would have perfected Malebranche's
tradition, he who, as it has been said, "Christianised
philosophy ;" while they would have reunited every
science to this Christian philosophy. Such men
would have known how to reconcile the true genius

of Christianity with philosophy and science. They
would have accepted in its true sense that great inspiration of harmony and unity which God set before
the mind of man in the first quarter of this century,
and which Germany has so abused.

I believe that our Fathers would have done this.
If we have not their talents, at least we may strive to
emulate their patience, their labour, and their good
will.

IV.

But the Oratoire did not only aim at intellectual
association.   It more specially contemplated the
organization of the secular priest's life, whatever might
be his individual vocation.   "If you are capable of
deep study " (so writes one of the earliest Oratorians)
" the Oratoire will provide you with quiet, with books,
and with pulpits from whence to teach.   If you seek
retirement, it offers you solitude as well as more busy
positions ; if you yearn after a life of penitence, you
will find men among us as ascetic as the Carthusians
themselves ; or if you are consumed by zeal for God's
service, our society offers you a choice of missions
and cures.   Do you delight in music and a splendid
ritual ? you can follow such.   In a word, the Oratoire
charitably moulds herself to every community, without becoming identical with any, inasmuch as it is not

separated from the Bishops, and is bound to all natural superiors."[1]

As to Henri Perreyve, I have already said what was that he sought in the Oratoire. His perpetual aim was "the more excellent way," and, therefore, following S. Paul's precept, he "coveted earnestly the best gifts," above all that whereby we "speak unto men to edification and comfort." He cared less to obtain a scientific mastery over truth than to enter within the glow of its brilliant beauty, with all its power to move, to kindle, and to comfort men. And that which chiefly drew him to join the infant society was that he saw in the Oratoire a school of love to mankind, a spot where the main science to be cultivated was a knowledge of the poor, of every fellow creature suffering in body or mind, of all classes of society who endure, or who seek, and, finally, the all important science which would teach us how to carry the Gospel of Christ to all such. What fervent eagerness used to be displayed in those weekly conferences, which Henri himself describes in his sketch of Hermann de Jouffroi, who was an extern of our union.

"These conferences were held every week, in the room of one of the Fathers, and their object was simply to discuss the working classes, the poor, the

[1] Oratoire de France, p. 95.

outcasts of this world ; and to seek some remedy for
their woes.   How eloquent Hermann used to wax,
how full his heart was, how like in tone to the Heart
of our Dear Lord, the poor man's true King ! how
powerfully he used to set forth convictions which come
into sharp collision with the world's pride, and jar upon
its selfishness."

Henri speaks of his friend, but his words are
equally applicable to himself, as again when he goes on
to say, " Hermann sought with all the power of his
noble soul to pour out a double portion of the Gospel
mind into all laws and regulations of human society."
But he contemplated this furtherance of an alliance
between heaven and earth with the utmost wisdom,
with well disciplined zeal, and with total freedom from
commonplace utopianism, while at the same time he
vigorously set forward the meaning of that primary
root of all Evangelizing, " Thy Will be done on earth as
it is in Heaven."   It was he who, seeking to strengthen
some among us who were out of heart, brought to light
some startling passages of S. Chrysostom, in which
that great Father ventures to tell every Christian that
he is responsible for the whole world, bidding each to
labour as far as in him lies to make earth more like
Heaven.   Moreover, Henri perfectly understood that
all such zeal must be " according unto knowledge ;"
and that in the present day we specially need to infuse

the Spirit of Christ's Gospel into the study of history, law, morals, politics, and political economy.

V.

Yes, this is the spirit which we must strive to infuse into the Oratory, if, as we hope, it is to live and expand. Amid the many clouds looming over our political and social life, is it not specially needful that those minds which are free from the whirl of passion should seek to cast a clear and peaceful light upon the stormy darkness? And as of old men whose lives were spent in contemplation meditated deeply upon the soul as seen in the Light of God's Presence, would it not be well that our modern contemplatives (if so be indeed that there are any such) should meditate profoundly upon human society, as viewed in that same Light? The most fertile source of all our ills is that scourge of hatred and wrath which has been ever waxing stronger during the last century. How blessed and glorious were that truly evangelic toil which should devote itself to the overthrow of wrath and hatred! What is there which so greatly divides the minds of men as division of heart? Surely he who can but ever so little lessen these wild gloomy influences among us would let in a flood of light upon the human mind. I am morally convinced that in all branches of the Church of Christ, in every school of philosophy (those only excepted which wilfully reject the light of reason), there are thousands of men who are kept back from a full faith, solely by the darkness which springs from the fierce passions aroused by strife.   Is it impossible to bring a new element into the contest—that of loving kindness, that absolute law of charity which is the characteristic of all which comes of God?

Could not Christ's commissioned writers ("ecce ego mitto ad vos scribas") introduce a hitherto untried method of polemics, one conformable to the Gospel of Love, one founded upon those Divine precepts, "Blessed are the peacemakers;" "Blessed are the meek, for they shall inherit the earth;" "Whosoever shall say to his brother, thou fool, shall be in danger of hell fire;" "Whosoever shall strike thee on thy right cheek, turn to him the other also;" "Be ye like to your Heavenly Father, who maketh His sun to rise on the just and on the unjust"?

It may be that the day will come when such will be the tone of priestly warfare.   Perhaps the Oratoire, if its offshoots spread and organize priestly life among us, will set the example.   A letter written to Henri Perreyve says,[1] "Are you firmly convinced of one thing, *cher enfant*, namely, that if ever any part of our work should take the shape of a course of publi-

---

[1] This letter is in fact written by the Père Gratry himself.

cations, the most essential character of all our studies and discussions must be perfect gentleness and charity? Nothing is more difficult; one might well-nigh say impossible. It is easy to make a very mild beginning, and one's first words may overflow with honey. But as soon as contradictions, misunder-standings, ignorance, dishonest opposition, blind or fierce passions arise, we kindle with what may at first be a repressed indignation, and before long it bursts forth. Well then, let us make a compact, let us help one another, by dint of good resolutions, to resist what seems almost inevitable. Granted that we meet with unfair opponents; we will not ever suppose our-selves to be addressing them; we will always turn to men who honestly seek the truth, and so doing, the most absolute meekness is not only a duty, but it be-comes our most powerful weapon.

"Will our ministers of the Gospel never be able to enter upon a solemn polemical and apologetic work in the spirit of S. Francis de Sales, who bore with every conceivable contradiction, annoyance, and insult, as Jesus Himself bore His buffetting, ending by a complete victory of Divine power through gentleness and perfect patience? Yes, indeed, *cher enfant*, therein lies a power as yet untried, a Divine power which Saints have truly wielded, but which authors, as yet, have not used. But be sure that if there are

any writers who bear Christ's mission ('ecce ego
mitto ad vos scribas'), they will go forth in that
strength. I am firmly convinced that if we had
courage always to take this line, if by dint of willing
and asking it of God, we could learn never to be dry,
or hard, or, what is far worse, ironical and sardonic ; if
we could acquire the art of finding some minute particle of reason in the most utterly unreasonable
antagonist ; if we sought for such with a view to
adopt and commend it, even as the analyst seeks
amid extraneous substances for a fraction of gold ;
if with all our light and knowledge we could be
imperturbably evangelical, meek as the Lamb of God,
then I truly believe that we might work miracles.
Every one who believes the Gospel, all friends of
justice and reason, would side with such true lovers of
peace. But then we must have absolute, unfailing
patience. Perhaps we may be meek towards our
avowed enemies ; but if our friends wound us, if our
own troops fire upon us, what then ? Are we to be
equally patient with such unexpected foes ?

"Yes, we must still be meek. If an altogether lawful and holy indignation kindles within you, you must
let it pour forth through prayers and tears, but not
through your pen. Do you understand all this, *mon
enfant bien aimé ?* Do you altogether and heartily
accept it ?"

I think Henri did most heartily accept and practice it. Young as he was, he knew how to write and speak without ever wounding any soul of man. Let him speak for himself, in the following passage :—[1]

"Meekness is strength; and it is all the more important to establish this truth, that many men, confounding meekness with weakness, mistrust this grace as an enervating power, and revile it most unjustly. Indeed, nothing is more common amongst us than to hear whispered accusations of concessions, tampering with error, enfeebled faith, even cowardice and treachery, and that to such a degree that it is a work of danger in our day to plead the cause of this much abused virtue. But I appeal to the doctrine of the Saints; and while but now we found S. Bernard interpreting the Saviour's words, 'Blessed are the meek, for they shall inherit the earth,' as meaning that God will give the grace of self-empire to a meek soul; so, turning to S. Chrysostom, he sets before us in that promised land of gentleness the gift of winning souls and conquering mankind. How is it that the meek shall inherit the earth, that great Saint asks? And he answers himself, 'Because it is theirs to conquer as many kingdoms as there are human hearts. For my part,' he goes on to say, 'I know nought so forcible or so irresistible as gentleness. We must needs

[1] Sainte Clotilde. Panégy., p. 421.

argue with the Gentiles or the foes of the faith with a true spirit of indulgent charity, for charity is all powerful to convert:' and elsewhere he says, ' Let us blush to assault our foes with the violence of wolves. Let us rather be as lambs, and we shall be conquerors, however numerous our enemies. If we take the part of wolves, we are sure to be overthrown, for the Divine Shepherd will forsake us :' and again, he says, ' Open wide the nets of charity, put forth the tender bait of mercy that you may draw your brother from out the gulf. Point out to him his errors and prejudices in the spirit of charity. If he will hearken to your voice, he is won ; if he resists, do not you be guilty of harshness, but argue with patience and meekness, lest the Sovereign Judge call you to account for his soul.' What solemn Christ-like words, how full of His Mind Who would not break a bruised reed, or quench the smoking flax !

" Why, indeed, should I seek the doctrine of the Saints, when the Saviour Himself has vouchsafed to say all that can be said on this weighty subject, and to confirm His words with His Example ? Open the Holy Gospel where you will, and at every turn you find the precepts of meekness, condemnation of all violent dealings with men's souls, promises of victory to perfect charity. All His sacred teaching bears the same stamp. There is nothing to justify the slightest harshness, the least tendency to override honour or the rights of conscience ; nothing to sanction apostolic zeal in 'proud, overbearing language, sharpness or disdain, fierce or contemptuous strength,' (I am quoting Bossuet[1]), such as are too often used by unwise servants of Christ, 'who, carried away by self-will, make a religion of their zeal, rather than draw zeal from their religion,' according to Bourdaloue." [2]

It was with such a mind that Henri Perreyve made ready to go forth to the conquest of souls.

VI.

I have not said all I might say of his preparation for the Priesthood. I have said nothing of his theological studies, or of the blessing which he shared in common with the rest of our first Oratorians, namely, the instructions of perhaps the ablest of all professors of theology[3]—one whose humility has ever shrunk from observation ; his comprehensive acquirements a marvel, yet always working to extend them ; his world contained in the narrow cell he seldom leaves ; his only earthly companions his books and his crucifix,

[1] Élévation sur les Myst. XIII. Serm. 4.

[2] Sermon pour le dimanche dans l'Octave de l'Ascension : —Sur le Zèle.

[3] The R. Père Gilet.

and that Father Who seeth in secret—" Pater qui es
in abscondito ; "—a man who with all his vast science
and prodigious memory never thought he was giving
sufficient time to the preparation of his lectures for
the few young men who composed his class—men
who still preserve their professor's notes as an un-
exhausted mine of theology. God reward him for
his zealous labours, and for all that he did to promote
the first beginnings of the Oratoire. He supplied our
little band with the most profound theological science,
as did another with the most striking lessons, both in
word and action, of practical piety and holiness.

Such was the blessed preparation Henri made for
his Priesthood, and the scene of that preparation was
as an abiding home, an intellectual household, a shrine
of holy friendship, in short, it supplied that great
need, the organization of his life.

" I cannot be sufficiently grateful for God's order-
ings," he says. " He paved the way before committing
His work to us, by drawing us into the close bonds of
friendship ; we were one in heart before we became
one in the Priesthood, and we are really one family
even as the world counts such ties. So soon as God's
Will is made known to any one of us the light is forthwith spread abroad among hearts so united as ours."

All this was fully realized. They lived and worked
together, loving, encouraging one another, each pro-

moting the other's preparation for his sacred calling. But after two years of this most happy and profitable life, it was forcibly interrupted in Henri Perreyve's case, and all his bright hopes seemed dashed for ever. It was not so in truth. Rather it was the way ordered of Providence to place him in a higher school—that school of suffering wherein God Himself is the sole Teacher. One morning there came another severe attack of hemorrhage, and Henri's life was in extreme danger. Yes indeed, this was his most real training for the Priesthood, for it was during those years of suffering and trial—borne as they were with the most unfailing courage—it was after an altogether unlooked for restoration to life, that he learnt God's lesson, which he himself renders thus : "My son, it is not for thyself that the renewed gift of life is bestowed on thee. This life which is restored thou owest it to mankind for My glory."

Death, which he had thus met face to face for the second time, burst any narrowing bonds which might still have fettered his soul, and set before him in a plainer light than ever the simplicity to which all things may be reduced. He no longer heeded anything save man's salvation and God's Glory. And herein he attained the true priestly mind: he was ready to begin his ministry.

Note to Chapter III.

Some most interesting remarks on the subject of the education of the clergy will be found in the "*Oratoire de France*" by P. Adolphe Perraud, in which he does not hesitate to grapple with the difficulties of our times. "We are passing through a period which is torn asunder in every direction by the most turbulent passions," he says: "There was a time when the priest's position and influence in society were accepted as a matter of course, but now everything is subject to doubt and criticism, above all what concerns the rights, teaching, and the government of the Church. The humblest parish priest is liable to encounter self elected *esprits forts;* and many on all sides reject the authority of his ministry. . . . . If we would do good among men, and set forward the salvation of their souls, in spite of prejudice and estrangement, it is obvious that we must seek elsewhere that authoritative *prestige* without which our words will be fruitless, our ministry ineffective. . . . . At the present time, fresh from the storm of revolution which casts men upon an unknown future, without guide or restraint, is it not evident that the Priesthood has new duties to fulfil, and that the necessity of the actual moment imposes a higher standard of duty than before upon all priests who are worthy of the name? The priest must always, everywhere, under all conditions, be a man of prayer and self-sacrifice. . . . . But if above all, and before all, he is called upon to be a man of eternity, as God's representative, he must most assuredly be also a man of time, inasmuch as his mission is to enlighten and heal the men of his time. If our Lord Jesus Christ had become Incarnate in the present day, or if He had selected any other country rather than Judea for the scene of His Incarnation, He would, we cannot doubt it, have adopted the garb and spoken the language of the people among whom He manifested Himself. Even so, if we would be understood by our contemporaries, and carry the words of everlasting life to their hearts, we must learn to speak their language. . . . . But this keen appreciation of the times we live in, this delicate capacity for being all things to all men without ceasing to be oneself, *i.e.*, God's Priest; this minute knowledge of the passions, the errors, the moral and intellectual evils of the day, all these are indispensable elements of modern ecclesiastical education, without which our ministry will fail to retain its hold over the faithful, or to win back the wandering sheep. Our soldiers are being armed with new weapons, and new machinery adapted to the novel practices of modern war and modern tactics; and in like manner God's soldiers must be furnished with fitting arms for the novel warfare they have to encounter, if they are to contend successfully against the passions and weaknesses of the day. Our rising generation of priests must not be content to seek a spirit of prayer, a habit of self-denial, a pure single-minded faith;—they must seek also the keenest apprehension of the special needs of our times. If ever there was cause to warn our younger brethren against that fatal delusion of indolence or inexperience which represents the ministry as a peaceful office in which a man may lead a tranquil, easy life, it is now. . . . . The priest of our day is often cast amid a population hostile to his teaching, mistrustful of his intention, merciless to his weaknesses, incapable of being won otherwise than by the genuine ascendancy of his own character combined with indefatigable self-devotion and the tenderest charity. We must await daily, hourly contests, we must always be able to prove our right to be believed or even tolerated; we must give no opening for blame, whether in the pulpit or the confessional, in our daily intercourse with the sick and poor, in our dealings with science and intellect, down to the most trifling details of external conduct and manner. Sceptical as the age is as regards our dogmas, it is unflinching in its judgment as to all that concerns the virtue or the dignity of the priest. With a rigid severity which would indicate a hidden instinct of that faith he has forsaken in practice, the worldly man will not tolerate common worldliness among priests. He is not content with the low secular standard ; —one might almost say that in proportion as he rejects the supernatural character of the priestly mission, so does he seem jealous of the priest's personal dignity of life. . . . Those who have to deal with clerical education must teach our young men to aim at tenfold courage, a tenfold spirit of faith and sacrifice ; to be real apostolic teachers, humble, charitable, ever ready to devote themselves to God's work ; but meanwhile, they must learn to see that social system amid which they will have to work in its true colours ; they must become acquainted with its dangers as well as its resources, its weak as well as its grand side—so as to be able to make a right use of the one, and not be disheartened by the other. . . . . . *Oratoire de France,* p. 414.

CHAPTER IV.

I.

AMID the endless diversity of gifts, of labour and of ministries, which alike set forward the service of God and man in Christ's Church, it was easy to foresee which Henri Perreyve would choose to follow. He was sure to aim at the highest : he was destined to follow S. Paul's precept, " Covet earnestly the best gifts, but rather that ye may prophesy." The Apostle tells us what he means by the gift of prophecy; it is the gift of " speaking to men unto edification and exhortation and comfort." This was to be his ministry ; this was the gift entrusted to him of God.

How marvellous are God's dealings with the hidden life of the soul, if we did but know how to perceive them ! Henri joined a class of theology, his soul full of longings, full of energy. A few of " God's students " met to meditate together upon the Gospel, one of the elder among them undertaking to guide the rest, and, as a result, Henri wrote : " Among these there is one poor weakly soul which tremblingly

accepts the truth, and gives itself to God. I give myself to Thee, O Lord Jesus Christ, to be used as Thou
wilt, in serving the poor brethren whom we love, in
turning souls from their false ideals, in doing good to
men. This it is which this frail soul cries out aloud,
and it is such a loving cry, so full of hopes, so full of
tears ! Ah ! indeed, I fain would do great things, but
I am nothing, and I can do nothing !"

Surely here is an instance of answered prayer. This
young fellow, hidden in a lowly community, unknown
to the world, asks for mighty things, and obtains them.
He obtained more than ambition, glory, or genius
has dreamt of : he obtained something of the gift
of prophecy—the sacred gift of teaching and comforting men. His prayers were answered through ten
years of vigorous energy amid suffering ; and won
at so costly a price, the Comforter Himself vouchsafed to entrust a portion of His Own inspiring gifts
to His servant. Henri's life was brief, but he raised
up and comforted many souls ; and when he died, he
left words of light and warmth behind him, which will
yet comfort and kindle and sustain many more. He
did a nobler work than the most glorious secular
task ; following in his Master's steps, he was a true
benefactor of mankind. He was one of those vigorous
workmen who uphold the Cross of Christ and the life
of God in the midst of the world and its nations.

II.

God permitted Henri to leave behind some words
of light and warmth, which have lifted up and comforted many a soul; which will not cease to do so.
And this I say more especially of his principal work,
"La Journée des Malades," a book which, if I am not
mistaken, will live long. It has all the enduring
qualities of deep thoughtfulness, exceeding simplicity.
and solid weight, which constitute a lasting work.
The truth is that it is a reality, called forth from the
very life of the writer. His brief Preface sets this
before us :

"This book has been written, *cher malade*, to comfort, strengthen, and cheer you amid the tedium of
sickness or convalescence. It has but one recom-
mendation, namely, that it is no set undertaking, it
is simply the result of a long personal experience of
the subject treated. Everything has been tried before
it was written."

Assuredly if there is any one thing which the author
tried and fully experienced during his long illnesses,
it was the ceaseless patient struggle to work on in
spite of suffering ; it was that trusting courage which up-
lifts the body by means of the soul, and the soul by the
help of God. Many of us watched him through one most

marvellous recovery—one which Henri himself con-
sidered as a very special blessing from God's Hand,
although he did not really know how exceedingly im-
minent his danger was.   But he knew by personal
experience how God does restore body and soul, and
his own history is told in the chapter entitled, "Courage
et travail."

" The soul wields the body, and makes it live and
breathe as it wills.   All strong passionate desire,
whether that of glory, knowledge, or even the mere
passionate search after pleasure, gives the soul this
wonderful empire over the senses.   One passion alone
should possess our souls, Christian brethren, that of
ceaseless unwearying toil to promote the coming of
Christ's Kingdom, and the reign of truth.   Blessed those
souls—there are such—in whom this passion absorbs
all others, taking the place of every longing, of ambition, science, pleasure, happiness itself.   Souls such
as these, while serving God and man, become the
very embodiment of will, courage, toil, sacrifice : they
never pause to consider wearily that strength fails and
death draws near ; they forget self utterly, they offer
themselves, they willingly give up their lives for the
Gospel, and, losing the low life of self, which degrades
and sullies so many souls, these find that true life
promised by the Saviour, that broad, generous, fruitful
life which finds its reward even in this world, through

the greatness of its works, the unexpected fulness of
its joy.

"Who can tell the happiness of work, I mean Christian work, done in the spirit of sacrifice, given to God,
carried on in His Sight? who can measure the fulness
of such work, even though he has tasted deeply of
it? Such work, though at first no more than a victory
over the weakness and reluctance of the body, will
speedily become its very healing."

All this I have seen heroically carried out in
Henri's own life.

But he drew the depth of his powers of consolation
from his own keenest trial, the whole course of which
is familiar to me, and which he bore, leaning on his
Dear Lord, with even more fervent courage than his
bodily sufferings.   Turn to that wondrous chapter,
"Le Crucifix:"

"Lord, the hour has come, the time of trouble, and
my soul knew not how to meet it.   I felt my whole
inner strength yielding beneath a burden of bitterness
too heavy for me to bear; a very flood of tears welled
up ready to drown my soul.

"Affrighted at the intensity of my own anguish, I
sought for aid; I looked wildly around, as though the
very weight of suffering must call forth some comforter.
But I was alone, and there was none to comfort
me.

" Then, O Lord Jesus Christ, I saw Thy Form, and
the instinct of healing drew me towards It ; I seized
It with a quivering hand, and bowed down my tear-
stained face upon It.   Many tears have been shed
over Thine Image, O Crucified Saviour !   It has power
to attract the tears of men, for there is a never failing
kindred between Thy Cross and all human suffering.

" Amid my tears I gazed upon Thy Hands, pierced
for love of men ; my lips were pressed to the nails
which held Thy Feet, and as I held Thy Cross my
hand grasped the sacred Wound of Thine Heart.
What said I ?   What did I hear ?   Not even in my
own heart can I tell ; but for long I abode in close
union with Thee ; I kissed Thy Wounds ; I clung to
Thy thorny Crown ; I drank deeply of Thy Cross ; I
bathed with tears that Cross which Thou didst bathe
with Thy Blood.   No strength had I to utter one
word ; but far down within my soul the words which
Thou Thyself didst utter in the extremest moment of
anguish rose up silently, ' Father, into Thy Hands I
commend my spirit.'   The echo of these sacred words
filled every hidden depth within me, lingering and
penetrating my life.   And then came peace.   I seemed
to fall asleep upon Thy Heart, and by degrees Love
overcame suffering.

" A strange, unhoped-for consolation, which I knew
was not from within, gently overflowed my soul, and

while I was yet marvelling at such unforeseen comfort, it waxed so mighty as to be well nigh like to joy.

"I still wept, but my tears were turned to tears of joy, and forgetting the irritable murmurs which even now burst from me, there rose up an involuntary hymn of thanksgiving. Calm strength returned. I felt myself girded anew to the strife; I felt that my will had been steeped seven-fold in the Blood of the Lamb."

Reader, these words are a simple record of facts; I know them to be such. God grant, that if ye who read ever taste the like desolation, akin to despair, ye may also taste the like unfailing reality of consolation.

III.

Such words as these, which really are more Henri's life than his mere writings, will suffice to show how largely he possessed the gift of "exhortation and consolation." God had indeed poured in upon him that grace which S. Paul calls the greatest of all (*meliora charismata*), as also that gift of prophecy which is—I reiterate it advisedly—the gift of "speaking to men to edification and exhortation and comfort."

Henri possessed in a most rare degree that sacred art of speaking to men, to every one his own language clearly and intelligibly, and hence arose the universal success of his public speaking, be his audience

what it might.   His words had the same power to
win, to enlighten, to comfort, to lead Godwards men
of the highest intellectual class, as the most ignorant
catechumen.   The result of his Conferences at the Sorbonne upon the highest class of listeners as to mental
calibre, was such that I have heard one of the greatest
living orators, and best qualified · judges, exclaim
enthusiastically, "Those who have not heard Perreyve
have no idea what human eloquence really is !"

There lies before me a carte de visite of Montalembert, left by him upon the Abbé Perreyve, after one
of these Sorbonne Conferences, and on it is written in
pencil, "I cannot get in ; but I must tell you that
I have been touched and kindled as I have not been
for twenty years—not since he of whom you are
the worthy successor used to enchant my youthful
mind at Notre Dame."[1]

Still greater to my mind was his success at the
Lycée Saint Louis, and above all at the Collége de
Sainte Barbe.   I doubt whether during the nineteenth
century any other priest in France has attained an
equal power of dealing with that most difficult of all
audiences—boys and young men.

---

[1] "Mon ami, on me refuse l'entrée.   Mais je veux vous dire
que je suis ému et ravi, comme je ne l'ai pas été depuis vingt
ans, depuis que celui dont vous etes le digne successeur enivrait
ma jeunesse à Notre Dame."

All those lads understood Henri Perreyve because
he spoke to them in their own language. And, bear
in mind,—to speak thus is a gift of the Holy Spirit ;
" audiebat unusquisque lingua sua illos loquentes."
The Spirit of love is familiar with every tongue, in
virtue of the same law which makes a mother able to
talk to her new-born babe. Henri felt such love,
such respect (he has often spoken of it to me), such
high ideas of the possible future of each one of these
souls, such value for the hidden treasures of every
heart among them, that practically he held the key
which can unlock them, and as soon as he appeared
among them they recognized a friend.

I shall never forget the description given to me of
one of his Conferences at the Lycée Saint Louis. He
was handling a most delicate and difficult subject,
and did so entirely in a narrative form. He told his
listeners the history of a death which he had wit-
nessed, and the crime which had caused that death.
Those who heard it will remember it all their lives ;
they will never forget how he described the meek,
innocent victim, or the guilt which could not be
reached by human law. And when Perreyve burst
forth, " This man, forsooth, is esteemed a respectable
man, honourable, upright, it may be even religious !
Messieurs, will you be content with such honour, such
religion? " there rose a thrill which pierced to the

depth of all present. Many of those young men were seen to shed tears, and after the Conference was over, they came crowding round him, with thanks, and the assurance, " You have opened our eyes for ever ! "

Henri's beginning at Sainte Barbe was not auspicious. In 1862 the Director begged him to give a Conference on every alternate Sunday morning, to the pupils of the Preparatory School and of the College. A certain innovation of the customary hours of freedom was involved, than which usually no greater grievance can be inflicted on schoolboys ! It was under these difficulties that the new preacher first appeared among some thousand listeners, all more or less aggrieved at their position. But scarcely had they met his glance, heard his voice, and listened to his first words, than a mighty change came over them ; the most lively attention was excited ; it was evidently a most welcome surprise to the lads, and the next day the pupils of the *grand Collège* sent the following letter to the *Préfet des Études*, to beg that the fortnightly Conferences which they thought such a burden but two days since might if possible become weekly.

" *Monsieur le Préfet*,—The pupils of the *grand Collège* beg you to thank M. l'Abbé Perreyve for his beautiful sermon on Sunday. Can they more fully express their gratitude than by begging him to give these Conferences which interest them so exceedingly, every week? Perhaps M. l'Abbé Perreyve's health and numerous engagements will not allow him to grant our request, but anyhow he may rest assured of our gratitude for his earnestness ; and for his striking and to us most helpful words.

"Sainte Barbe, Tuesday, March 11th, 1862."

(Here follow the signatures.)

IV.

This unrivalled success among all audiences, and specially this most difficult one, is to be explained by S. Paul's teaching in his marvellous treatise on preaching, which we read in the xii., xiii., and xiv. chapters of the First Epistle to the Corinthians.

The great Apostle bids those whose office it is to teach not to speak to men in *an unknown tongue.* "He that speaketh in an unknown tongue speaketh not unto men, but unto God . . . he edifieth himself," but not the Church ; he speaks, but no man hears—*nemo enim audit.*

What does this mean? what is this unknown tongue, which nevertheless is a gift of God (xii. 10, 11), which speaks to God (xiv. 2), which puts forth the mysteries of the Spirit—*.Spiritu autem loquitur mysteria* (xiv. 2), which edifies him who speaks (xiv. 4), and yet which "no man understandeth"

(xiv. 2)? What language is this? The answer is plain. It is the Sacred Word itself, which does indeed set forth the doctrine and the mysteries of the Spirit, and is understood of God, but which men neither understand nor listen to. "I have set forth the truth," says a preacher who has spoken this unknown tongue. "Men have not listened; it is their own fault." Yes, he says truly, and men are wrong not to learn that language in which he has been speaking. But listen once more to S. Paul: "Let him that speaketh in an unknown tongue pray that he may interpret"—*oret ut interpretetur* (xiv. 13). "I had rather speak five words with my understanding," the Apostle goes on to say, "than ten thousand words in an unknown tongue" (xiv. 19).

Of a truth it is not enough to preach the mysteries of Christianity through mere formulas, which albeit true before God, are not readily understood. The real Apostle and Prophet is he who has the gift of interpreting those deep and hidden formulas, of adapting them to every period and every mind. What S. Paul calls "interpreting the unknown tongue," is translating the sacred language of hidden mysteries into ordinary words, as Jesus Christ Himself put forth truths which had been hidden from the foundation of the world in parables; it is to frame the living word anew with every age, suiting it to the needs of that age, without departing from the venerable antiquity of truth. But the very first condition of knowing how to do this as the Gospel requires is a knowledge of the times in which we are living—" Hoc autem tempus quare non probatis:" it is to know that the Eternal Word is Monarch of all ages, and that no time, no people, no soul of man can ever be devoid of this inspiration ; that every man and every age has at this very actual moment an aim, a vocation, a mission, which the masters of the interior life call *the order of the present*,[1] and that this really means that actual Will of our Hidden God—*Pater qui es in abscondito*—which every age and every man bears about within him. Now it is exactly this Hidden God, Present as He really is in all times and to all minds, whom the Christian prophet is bound to announce and reveal to every age and every man, even as S. Paul revealed Him to the Athenians. I know well that the false spirit of the age, corrupt and corrupting, blinds men in every season, and that this is precisely the veil or rather the winding sheet which is thrown over our Hidden God. But this same God Who dwelleth in the hidden places is the Source of life, the Ideal, the Inspiration which kindles every heart and every age to tear the veil, to cast aside the

---

[1] " L'ordre du moment présent."

cerecloth, and to fill all things living with light, strength, power, and gladness.

And how, when you come to the detail of preaching, how are you to make this man or this age love God, save by teaching him to see the Hidden God within him ; that is to say, the ideal which he very likely abuses, and that action of Providence which possibly is disturbed by his irregular efforts? Above all, how are you to win the youth of any period save by that very *élan* which fills and stirs it? All our highest ideal is God : all action has its source in God. Surely then, it is possible to bring back every ideal and every action to Him.

This much granted, let us apply it to our own age; if that age is engrossed by an irresistible movement, and a universal cry, wherein we may distinguish the words liberty, equality, progress, is it hard to discern the working of our Hidden God, or to discover His Voice in that of the people? Is it so hard to turn that cry for liberty to the liberty of the children of God, which S. Paul alleges to be the aim of all this world's progress, the only means, indeed, thereof? "The whole creation waiteth for the manifestation of the sons of God ; it groaneth under the bondage of corruption, for the glorious liberty of the children of God."[1]

[1] Rom. viii.

And again, is it so hard to recall the cry of liberty to those primitive notions of Christian liberty, of moral and religious liberty, of the liberty of the soul to resist vice, error, concupiscence, and pride; the soul's holy liberty in God, without which even our adversaries have proved that all advance in liberty, whether civil or religious, political or international, is an absolute impossibility?

Is it so hard to apply to modern times those words of the Saviour and Deliverer, Who replied to certain slaves of the law who believed themselves to be free, "Whosoever committeth sin is the servant of sin. . . . If the Son shall make you free ye shall be free indeed"?[1] Or is it so difficult to bring back the cry of equality to the *fiat æqualitas* of S. Paul, or to that wonderful letter of S. James, which may be called the Epistle of Equality? Is it so hard to realize that the Divine Mission of the age now beginning is practically to attain that phase foretold by the Lord Himself in His eternal law of progress, which, as yet, none have rightly understood,—"If ye continue in My Word ye shall know the truth, and the truth shall make you free"? This is the law of progress in all its phases. It means, whether generally of mankind. or individually, that if the Word of God, the Christian faith, dwells in us, then, and then only, all eternal

[1] John viii. 34–36.

knowledge of truth will be vouchsafed us, and through
this truth we shall attain to liberty.   Hence it follows
that the problem Christianity has to solve, since its
birth amid the ruin of the old world, is to attain
through faith to the knowledge of truth, and thereby
to the possession of liberty.   Such is God's Will ; it is
His doing ; it is the work of a Hidden God.   And so,
when I see my generation carried away by a movement which it cannot fathom, perpetually driven back-
wards for want of understanding, surely it is the time
to say with S. Paul, " Whom ye ignorantly worship,
Him declare I unto you."

It was precisely this which our dear friend did : it
was what Lacordaire and many another had done
before.   Henri himself appreciated Lacordaire's pro-
phetic *clairvoyance.*

" These few lines," he wrote, " contain Père Lacordaire's political programme.   The leading idea is the
union of religion and liberty, and the first practical
application thereof is a sincere, loyal, inviolable
attachment to those principles which the modern
world tries painfully but persistently to reconcile.
One might hesitate as to the means selected, but
there is no doubt as to the thing to be done.   Either
nothing can be done at all, or the attempt must be
made to reconcile modern society with the Gospel, by
proving that the primary laws of its existence, so far

from encountering an implacable foe in Christianity,
have really only come to light under the shelter of
Christian thought. It needed to show that political
liberty, if free from revolutionary licence and anarchy,
is dear to the Catholic Church, is actually one of its
stoutest earthly guarantees. One must convince this
modern society that the Gospel is the source of all
social progress, of all legitimate effort to lessen the
inequality of men's lots, the book *par excellence* of the
poor and lowly, without which all social reformation
can be but a dream, more or less bloodstained. And,
finally, it is necessary to explain that all secular intoler-
ance which would argue by means of the sword or
the law rather than by the ministry of the word, which
would convert men with the bayonet, so far from being,
as it has been affirmed to be, an article of the Catholic
faith, is an abominable doctrine, condemned by the
Church, abhorrent to all her saints. All these things
it was needful to say to the modern world, with a
perfect conviction, with a moderation and discretion
all the deeper because every human passion is on the
watch to stifle and overwhelm such really noble
thoughts."

Yes, indeed, this is what we have to do, or we
must plainly give up all idea of winning our age and
that which is to come. It is of no avail to go on for
generation after generation repeating eternal truths in

an unknown tongue ; " Nemo enim audit." We should dwindle away while so doing, ages and generations following on in their afar off course. Surely those men who refuse to translate these everlasting formulas into modern language, who will not preach the Unknown God Who is now ignorantly served by our people, who cannot speak that people's language, surely they prove this very fact ? They say that all is lost, that the ages as they flow on must fall deeper and deeper into the gulf—that none can draw them out. "The world is fast nearing its close," they say; "let us save our own souls ; let us raise our standard and die ; let us fall beneath the shadow of our Eternal *Credo.*"

Such men are very brave soldiers :—I have watched this gloomy, persistent courage even unto death in many a Christian heart; but it seems to me that it is not the truest form of heroism. It reminds me of the mournful heroism of the Apostle Thomas when, on hearing of Lazarus' death, he exclaimed, " Let us also go that we may die with him." I would rather choose the bright heavenly hope which said, " Our friend Lazarus sleepeth, let us go and awake him out of sleep."

You tell me that our existing world has been, Lazarus like, dead for the past four centuries. If so, need is that we say with our Lord in the Gospel, " Our friend Lazarus sleepeth ; let us go that we may waken him out of sleep." But truly our modern world is strangely

unlike Lazarus, who was silent and motionless in the
grave ; its tumultuous cries and restless agitation are
more akin to him that was possessed, he whose name
was Legion. And even so, cannot He Who overcame
the world drive out this Legion ? Yet, neither will
this simile hold good ; the world of our day is not
possessed ; within it there are two worlds, two ages,
two cities, and these two worlds are to be found in
every nation, well-nigh in every soul. It is a mere
panic to assert that the City of God is about to be
overthrown by that other power—a panic the very
existence of which I could not realize for long. But
at last I have explained it to myself as follows :—Men
with logical minds, and hearts full of faith, gaze upon
our modern world, carried away as it is by an irresistible movement. They see plainly that no power
can stop the rush, and that the more we oppose it, the
more we are trodden under foot. If then this movement is intrinsically perverse, if it arises from the city
of evil, it is plain that the world is lost, and the City
of God on earth is overthrown.

But I reply that this movement in our age is a sign
of the times which we ought to know how to read.
" Signa autem temporum non potestis scire." We must
analyse that active force, and search out the motive
power of such eager movement. Of course the First
Cause of all movement, without exception, is God.

And if so, we may start by saying that the first cause
of this contemporary movement is God.   It is God
Himself, it is our Lord Jesus Christ Who wills the
growing freedom of all men, of all nations in justice
and truth, and that with a will which becomes ever
stronger as the world goes on.   Unquestionably the
evil of our day perverts all heaven-sent movement in
a hundred ways, but we must resist the perversion,
not the movement itself.   And if any one thing is
certain, it is that we shall never overcome that perversion, save by means of the very movement itself,
and of its first principle, which is God; even as S.
Paul did not attempt to cast down the shrines of idols
save by setting up amid them the True God, Hidden
and Unknown.   I repeat it, the excessive discom-
fiture of those who are under a delusion as to the only
way of regaining the nations of earth is a striking
proof of what I maintain, namely, that we shall
be indefinitely thrown back, more and more overthrown, so long as, failing to enter into the signs of
the times, we persist in contesting, at one and the
same time, against the impetus which comes from
God and the passions which pervert that impetus;
so long as, in consequence, we do not learn to overcome, by means of that very Godsent impetus, the
perversion which man has wrought in it.   The day
will come when we shall learn this, even if we require

the lessons of three centuries of disaster and the almost total destruction of the Church first.

We must go on re-affirming the truth—that in order to enlighten our age, to set it free, to lead it back to God, we must imitate S. Paul, who shattered the idols behind which the Unknown God was concealed. Our age is full of idols of liberty, whereas the One True God of liberty has but scant altars, and upon these few you might but too truly inscribe the Apostle's words, " Ignoto Deo." Who among us realizes liberty— that liberty with which Christ has made us free? Who has any true understanding, any true love of real liberty? Where are the faithful followers of such liberty to be found?

Liberty indeed! You know somewhat of it in idolatry and superstition, " Quasi superstitiosiores vos video," but not in spirit and in truth. Yet in spirit and in truth alone can men rightly adore liberty, and such worship is what the world needs.

You answer that the time is not come for us to say to our age, " That which you ignorantly worship I declare unto you." Listen to me. You have lived too long already in the midst of a revolution which sweeps you along with its tide ; you can neither guide its course nor determine its end. You have entered upon a new stage of the world's history, of which it has been said that " Revolution is not an event, it is an epoch." One half of mankind cries out that Revolution is evil, the other half that it is just. Yes, indeed, the evil is idolatry; but true justice is to be found in the Unknown God, Whom I declare unto you. It is your part to disentangle these contradictions, to overthrow evil, and glorify justice; it is your duty, and your only safety. To INTERPRET REVOLUTION BY THE LIGHT OF THE GOSPEL, in wisdom, in peace, in fraternity, this is the problem of our day, the main task of all apostles of truth and prophets of liberty.

Henri Perreyve appreciated all this, he taught and practised it; it was thus that he was the man of his times and spoke the language thereof. He followed in the footsteps of S. Paul, of whom Bossuet says so strikingly, that " it is a characteristic of his Epistles that they are so vigorous and independent, so completely entering into the spirit of the age and of all that was stirring in it."[1] He had no mind to cast contempt on any of the watchwords of the day. There is a certain power in every watchword which men honour; it is as one of the strings of an instrument which soothes and instructs, which charms and comforts man. " Honour, reason, nature, country, courage, love, science, liberty, progress," why should any indignity be offered to such

---

[1] " Les Epîtres de Saint Paul, si vives, si originales, si forts du temps, des affaires, et des mouvements qui étaient alors ! "

noble words? Rather, O ye poets, prophets, apostles, be it yours to draw out their fullest, deepest meaning, that which is at once truest and most bewitching. To do this was the spirit of Henri Perreyve's ministry.

V.

I would ask you to follow out this assertion by reading Henri Perreyve's Preface to Lacordaire's Letters, wherein we trace how that noble, far-seeing man taught his cherished disciple the art of speaking to the men of his day.

"DEAR FRIEND,"—so Lacordaire wrote to Henri, "our country is lost if it is not won back to religion. There will be fresh movement doubtless, but all such stirrings will be fruitless until the land opens its eyes to that eternal Light which Jesus Christ sheds upon earth through the Gospel. You my son, are called to labour for this regeneration, and it is a thought which should comfort you through everything, or at least give you strength to endure everything. For my own part, it is an untold happiness to me that my conscience bears me witness that for seven and twenty years, from the day of my first consecration to God, I have not said a word or written a sentence the object of which was not to impart the spirit of life to France, and to impart it in an acceptable form, *i.e.,* with meekness, temperance, and patriotism. Some day you will do the like."

Henri did indeed do the like. In this same Preface he places the great religious and political problem of our day before the listening world of young men. " What may not be looked for from you, young men of this day," he asks, " if you accept the guidance of this religious inspiration, wisely and bravely?

" You will inherit a treasure the absence of which has deprived us to a cruel extent of peace and real greatness. You will be as the Christians of olden time in your new life; humble servants of God, and yet bold and free citizens; you will maintain the convictions of eternal truth, interpreted by the light of our modern intelligence; you will solve that mighty problem which a venerable voice but lately pronounced to be 'the problem of the age,'—the alliance of religion and liberty.

" Have you ever reflected upon the great destiny which, it may be, awaits you?

" When the work of destruction is finished in this trembling Europe; when the storm of revolution has destroyed all that God wills to perish; when the reckless hands that have done this deadly deed have themselves perished beneath the ruin they have wrought then will be the time to clean out the foundations of the Temple, and to rebuild its walls that it may be the blessing of the coming age. This day of great things depends upon you, young men. It is to you that the world will look. How will you dig those foundations in which the next century is to find safety? Oh beware, I beseech you, that you do not pave the way for more earthquakes, fresh ruin! Learn wisdom from the toil, the tears, the blood of your forefathers. Would to God that you may realize that the foundations of human society are sacred, and that it is not enough to insure the solid greatness of future generations, that you cast in your offering of gold, or birth, or progress, or even glory and genius. There is but ONE Corner Stone—'Hic est lapis.' All who have ever sought to build save on That Stone were swept away before the first storm blast; there is nought that can stand save It.

"'Turn to history. Whosoever has sought glory save through Him has only succeeded in letting loose the deadly spirit of battle strife upon the world.

"Whosoever has sought to make wealth apart from Him has only succeeded in brutalizing men, by turning immortal souls into a tortured, frenzied machine, toiling, blaspheming in its darkness.

"Whosoever has sought science without Him has been engulfed in the quicksands of false reasoning and vain criticism.

"Whosoever has clutched at power without Him

has been plunged amidst bloody revolutionary vic-
tories; and whosoever has sought liberty without
Him has waked up, throttled by a military force
which, while loading him with fetters, has derisively
asserted ' I am Liberty !'

"And all this because He of Whom I speak was
wanting! My friends, it is He Whom above all we
need to know, Whose Eternal Name must be graven
on the foundations of our future edifice. All that has
been great in the past was built upon that Divine
Name; and our present dangers and trials draw us to
It more than ever. Would that I had Lacordaire's
power to press it upon you :—' It is the Name of
Jesus Christ.'"

VI.

But with respect to Henri Perreyve's ministry of
the Word there remains yet one thing, and that the
best of all, to be told. Of a truth, all this would have
been worthless in my eyes if he had stopped short
therein. But filled as he was with the grandest of
ideals, he never believed himself to have attained
thereto. If earthly genius is wont to be dissatisfied
with its own choicest works, how much rather a noble
heart which loves and seeks after God, which toils to
build up the kingdom of eternal beauty upon all the
earth, and above all within itself? And herein the
essential, unfailing characteristic of truth is humility.

I have already said that when celebrating his first Mass, the day after his ordination, Henri asked three things of God ; and of these the first was, *grace to be a humble priest.* And truly his earnest, frank, sensitive, impetuous character did not fail to grow in humility all through a life made up of success, commendation, friendship, and affection.

We all know how difficult it is to persuade most people to endure any correction, any censuring judgment, or restraint. It was far otherwise with Henri. My perpetual cry to him was, " Seek recollection ; be recollected !¹ Your knowledge is not as extensive, or your mind as deep, as it might be. Unless you work hard, in the most recollected spirit, for years to come, you will abide as you are ; you will not become all that you might be." And his answer was, " It is perfectly true ; I see it. I will do as you would have me. I understand you thoroughly."

Among his letters one to the Abbé Ansault (an aumonier at Sainte Barbe) expresses a depth of humility for which I was scarcely prepared. At a time when he was living in a sphere of almost unlimited admiration he pronounced this unduly severe but most sincerely felt judgment upon himself :

" 'Thank you for all you have so kindly said of me. I can trace your indulgent affection in it. . . . At

---

¹ " Recueillez vous ! recueillez vous ! "

one time I feared you must have discovered a depth
of miserable pride in me. Alas ! . . . But as I knew
you better, this dreadful fear could not last ; you are
sincere ; you deserve that I should be equally so. I
must tell you, then, that I am quite alive to my intellectual position. I feel that I possess but a commonplace talent, which is now emitting its brightest
fire, and will be soon exhausted. I am not conscious
of anything deep or really original and powerful in
me. When my miserable name is mentioned in the
same category with that of Père Lacordaire or Ozanam
(I know not how, but it has been done several times
this year, even publicly) it gives me a feeling of
inward pain which I hardly know how to put into
words. If I were to affect to succeed such men I
should but prepare a most bitter disappointment for
myself during the next twenty years, should it please
God that I live so long ; for after the first fancy is
over, the public would take a truer view of things !
But, thank God, I have no such thought in my mind,
and all I ask of His Providence is that I be
enabled to do some little good in a necessarily very
inferior degree, both intellectually and scientifically,
to a few youthful minds which through me will pass
on to something higher than I. There is some danger,
dear friend, even in saying this to you ; for there is
such a thing as false modesty, and if I did not know

you so thoroughly, I might fear being suspected of it.
But, indeed, now I have the fullest trust in you.   So
do not praise me any more, and do not deceive me as
to myself.   Let us work, work, work ! we shall still
be quite sufficiently ignorant, weak, governed by the
popular prejudice and the little servile fears which
surround us.   May God look mercifully upon our
work, and grant us—inasmuch as this is the calling
He assigns us—grace to do some little service for His
Sake to these dear young fellows who are so earnest
in seeking His Word, who hunger and thirst so heartily
for His Gospel."

This most obviously humble and sincere judgment
of himself showed a clear view of the weak point
which would have developed in Henri, as in any other
man of his age, if he had ceased to work and seek
recollection ; if he had not striven perpetually to
strengthen and deepen his mind and soul.   It was
a judgment which might have been verified, though
it never was.   Possibly Henri Perreyve was for a
moment in danger ; but it could not last.   The difficulty had been conquered before death interposed.
And that victory was the greatest triumph of all which
were won by that most powerful, original, deeply
religious soul, blessed as it was of God to His own
special service

CHAPTER V.

AN IDEAL.

AS I have said, Henri Perreyve had framed for himself so noble an ideal of the ministry of the Gospel and the priestly life, that while he never, thank God, could rest satisfied with himself, he was ceaselessly aiming at an ever higher and higher standard of beauty and holiness of life. But once there seemed a risk of his halting, when the multitude of work and the distractions of an overstrained zeal disturbed the inward recollection of his life. I must return to this most serious cause of danger. But meanwhile I am enabled to study Henri's ideal of life; to trace out what filled his soul and kindled his heart when, being on the threshold of what he calls "my joy of joys, the sole object of my whole life," his priestly ordination, he was making ready for the weighty office in Retreat. Then, above all other seasons, he strove, by the most earnest, fervent meditation, to attain to what I have already called the transfiguration of courage and love. He then wrote down those promises to God which most truly shaped his after-life. He kept these notes, though no one ever saw them until after his death. Most sincerely do I thank him for the profit my own soul has gained from them. Brother Priests, you too will thank him and pray for him. And you, young men, in whose hearts works an ambition to become the benefactors of mankind, you will learn from him that there is no more practical self-devotion to be found than in the Priesthood. Or, if your career is already otherwise shaped, you will learn here that a certain sacerdotal tone of mind is to be sought and found by every man who would fulfil his appointed task on earth.

Let us see how Henri Perreyve looked upon the life and the death of Jesus Christ's priests.

The MS. is dated: "Retraite de Saint Eusèbe, Rome, 1857." It contains four meditations—Chastity, The Priest's Death, Persecution, Love of Man. I give the last three.

I.

The Priest's Death.

The Priest should look upon death as one of his sacerdotal functions: It is his last Mass. It is from this point of view, Lord, that I would fain meditate to-day upon death, at Thy Feet, before Thy Cross, before that bloodstained Cross whereon hangs the Saviour of the world. Strengthen Thou my heart, that it may bring forth much fruit.

Death: Reason is that I should often contemplate it ; first generally because I am a man, and death is the inseparable companion of man's life. We see it, we feel it daily ; it touches us through those we love before it lays its hand upon oneself and puts an end to all things, so far as this world goes. Moreover, I ought individually to meditate upon death because I am ill; because but a few days since, my frail life seemed passing away; because skilful doctors have declared that the cold hand is already upon me ; because I am conscious within myself of the presence, the working of those germs of death which undermine life, and sooner or later must inevitably overpower it. Further, I ought to contemplate death because I hope to be a priest ; and so to-day I will meditate upon it from the priest's point of view.

What, then, is death to the priest ?

O Incarnate Lord, Thou art the Priest of priests, the example of all Thy priests in all things, but if I seek to discover what in all Thy Life was the crowning act of Thy Priesthood, I see plainly that it was to be found in the hour of Thy Death. A Priest in the lowliness of the manger, a Priest in the Purity of Thy Life, a Priest in the penitence of the desert, a Priest

in the Sermon on the Mount, a Priest when instituting
Thy Sacraments, especially in the Holy Eucharist;
but more than any of these, a Priest upon the Cross.
This was the most solemn hour of Thy Priesthood;
the chief sacrifice, the essential act of Thy Pontificate.
That moment in which Thou bowedst Thy Head
and gavest up Thy Spirit to Thy Father, bidding death
do its worst, that was the act of consummation. All
was then finished, that moment saved the world.

I can perceive too clearly how Thou didst take the
form of man chiefly in order to accomplish this last
sacrifice, since although Thou didst use Thy fleshly garb
to teach men by Thy word and Thine example, Thou
couldst have revealed Thy secrets as before indirectly
through Thy Prophets, or directly, as through Moses
on Mount Sinai. But suffering and death required
human flesh to suffer and die, and thus death is the
great end, the sovereign object of Thine Incarnation.
That mortal body which Thou didst put on was never
to Thee, O Christ, other than the material of sacrifice, the means of suffering, of dying, and therein of
saving the world; Lord, even such should this mortal
body be to each man who is admitted to share Thy
Priesthood. Each man should use it, as Thou didst,
to preach the truth, to edify others by his example; to
succour the needs, the sorrows, the weaknesses of his
fellow men; to have pity upon all the many ills of

humanity, and that all the more in that he himself is
a partaker therein. But the essential, the sacerdotal
purpose to which it should be used is to die. Such
death must be begun in chastity, continued in mortification, consummated in that actual death, which is the
priest's final oblation, his last sacrifice. He should
make ready for death long beforehand, even as Thou,
Lord, foretold and dwelt upon Thy Death to Thy
disciples, long before Thy Passion.

Thy priests should prepare for death, as they prepare to celebrate Mass, for truly the death of a priest
is a Mass; a union with Thy Death, consummated with
Thine for the salvation of men.

They should offer it for the coming of Thy Kingdom
upon earth, for the increase of faith and hope among
men, for the world's salvation. They should behold
their deathbed as an altar, whereon to offer their
blood in expiation of sin, as the priest does when he
raises the chalice towards the Cross.

They should desire death even as Thou didst desire
Thy Passion, notwithstanding the anguish and terror
which Thou didst know awaited Thee, out of love of
God and love of man. What if Thy priests, O my God,
far from beholding death thus, look on it as a foe?
What if they fear it, shun it? if they dread its foreshadowing, its afar off sound, as though it were a fearful,
intolerable vision? What if, instead of counting death

as the most solemn of our festivals, the most worthy
sacrifice of our whole life, we fear it? Nevertheless,
when I examine myself, I detect some lingering traces
of this cowardly, unintelligent, heartless, heathenish
fear. The disturbance and danger which have lately
threatened my life, so far from tending to detach me
from it, have practically made me cling the closer, and
with a more hidden instinct, to it. I am more distressed, more dismayed at the reappearance of those
symptoms which are the forerunners of death. And
this it is, Lord, that I would now intreat Thee to blot
out, to put away from me. I feel that it is Thy Will,
and that Thou wilt do so if I can but ask it with
sufficient faith, trust, and love. O my God, Thou Who
hast transformed death by Thy sacerdotal and vic-
torious death, take from me all these fears. It is
that fear which is my chief foe, my main hindrance,
the heavy crushing weight which stifles all that is good
in me. Do Thou teach me to break this chain,
which galls me and keeps me from all free movement.
Cast me into what danger Thou wilt, into the midst
of contagion or political revolution—those anxious
turbid seasons when men's presence of mind is apt to
fail, and fear and evil join in a cowardly alliance.
At all such seasons grant me to find strength in a
bold, free acceptance of death. I have seen, Lord, and
sometimes I have even felt, that so doing, a man finds

perfect courage, perfect calmness, full and free command over his inner movements.

But this is not enough : I dare to ask yet more. It is hard not to fear death, if we view it on its fearful side ; it is easier to love it, inasmuch as it possesses a beautiful, an attractive side ; and I would fain view it from thence. And thus, Lord, I presume to ask of Thee grace to love death ; and since it is not well to be taken by surprise by the unforeseen approach of the grim shadow, I pray Thee that Thou wouldst fill my mind with a continual, incessant meditation upon death. I know, Lord, that so far from being saddened by such meditation, Thy Grace can enable me to draw thence a vigorous, cheerful freedom of heart. Teach me, Jesus, to become familiar with death, to look upon it as an obligation laid upon me by my priesthood, stern indeed, but lovely and fertile. Teach me to love it, even as Thou teachest men to love the sufferings of a pure life, the austere joys of mortification ; those joys which sweep over one as one lays one's anguish before the Crucifix—joys so inconceivable, so utterly frantic and delusive to the eye of carnal reason, yet so real, so actual to the soul that has sought to taste them for Thy Love's sake. These things are painful in themselves ; they would be insupportable were it not for love. But love has a boundless power of turning suffering into joy ! Teach me then to look at death solely in and through Thy Love.

Henceforth I would alter the turn of my thoughts on this subject; I would strive to betray no sign or shadow of terror in conversation, even in my most passing words, of death. Fear is infectious, and it were a terrible thing if Thy priests encouraged the fear of death among men. Alas, Jesus Christ my Lord, dare I say it all! Thou knowest my one desire, my one ambition, which I scarce dare utter, so unworthy is my weak cowardly heart thereof, so far beyond my worthlessness it is. But, Lord, Thou knowest how often, almost ceaselessly, here by the tombs of Thy martyrs, and when I receive Thy Precious Body, I have asked that I might shed my blood for the Faith, for Thy Love. I know, O Lord, that such a prayer is unfitting in such as I am, yet by the help of Thy Grace, may I not become less unworthy thereof, less unworthy to wash my sacerdotal robes in the Blood of the Lamb? Of a truth that were indeed a blessed day: " Beati qui lavant stolas suas in Sanguine Agni."

But if Thou wilt have me abide in my mediocrity, if Thou hast chosen for me a death void of visible grace and glory, a lowly death which has more terror for me than one more noble—languor, the slow painful extinction of youth which yet clings to life; yet, Lord,

I know that even so, such a death as that may bring forth fruit for the world's salvation. I know that the dying priest yet stands before Thine Altar, and that on his bed of anguish, as upon the scaffold, he may justly raise the sacrificial Psalm, " Introibo ad Altare Dei."

May these thoughts sink deeply into the depths of my heart. May Thy Grace vouchsafe to fix them there; above all reviving them with ten-fold force when the solemn hour of sacrifice comes; then may Thy Fatherly Hand uphold and guide me through the shadowy paths, wherein, O Christ, Thou hast left the track of Thy triumphal footsteps: "Qui sequitur Me non ambulat in tenebris."

II.

Persecution.

Lord, I know that these calm days of peace, this sweet and holy happiness which Thou hast granted me to taste here on Roman soil, beneath the shadow of S. Peter, will not last. Already are they well nigh over. Soon I must leave beautiful Rome, and return to France, and I do but half regret it, for after all, France is the rightful field for my toil and struggle, and I knew all along that these days of rest were given solely for the better gathering in of strength.

What destiny awaits us in France ? Thou, Lord,

Alone, knowest what the future has in store. But to human foresight there seems little hope of peace and prosperity. Righteous retribution, vengeance too justly irritated, seem impending, and in the day of wrath and blind revenge there will be no distinction made. And indeed such distinction would be an evil. Innocent victims are the saving of a good cause, and Thy Church has ever flourished when watered by her martyrs' blood; we need not ask to be the exception, and if we are less detested than some others we ought to use what little influence we have to save them, and maintain God's cause. By so doing we involve our own certain loss.

Of a truth, my God, the storm seems gathering : its first distant thunder was heard after that crime which carried bloodshed into the Church's bosom, and startled the whole world.

Men say that in France the clergy are insulted publicly, and the irreligious press, making the most of all such seeds of revolution, has recommenced an attack upon us which seems to be organized and permanent. Perhaps then a time of real persecution is looming, and it matters greatly that we be not taken by surprise. Suffer me, Lord, to meditate upon the thought before Thee, and teach me with what weapons to ward off the danger.

There are two forms of persecution : that of con-

tempt and that of violence. Mockery and the axe ;
ridicule and blood.

Contemptuous persecution is the hardest to bear
well. It is at once that which touches us most nearly,
and that for which we are least prepared. For long
we have lived under the *régime* of respect ; our garb,
our duties are held in honour ; we are for the most
part treated with consideration and delicacy by enlightened men. That is the character of the religious
movement of our day. But the people despise us.
And yet it is that very people whom we love specially !
Their contempt is unworthily fostered by a thousand
lies and calumnies, and by the used-up remains of
Voltairianism which have descended from the upper
classes to the lowest dregs of the nation.

We may, therefore, expect the era of contempt with
that of democratic revolution : we must look for it, and
acknowledge that the way for such a chastisement has
been paved by many a fault. We shall be insulted ;
the priest will once more be an object of ridicule and
odium ; we shall not be feared, perhaps scarcely
hated ; we shall be despised, that is all. A terrible
infliction, in facing which I feel most weak. What
are we to oppose to such persecution?

Two things above all else : Christian humility and
gentleness.

HUMILITY : accepting buffets, gazing upon Christ

in the prætorium, and willingly steeping ourselves in humiliation; blushing before God, so that we may have the less cause to blush before men; bowing ourselves to the earth before Him, and drinking of the bitter waters, that He may lift us up; "De torrente in via bibet, propterea exaltabit caput."

GENTLENESS: never growing irritated; no anger, pride, or haughtiness. Ah! dear Lord, many among us have been betrayed into using this manner of defence of Thy holy truth, of old unknown to Thy Church: they meet contempt with contempt; injury with injury; calumny with calumny. Proud and violent towards the violent, they give back threat for threat, and meet the persecutors who thirst for blood in a sanguinary spirit, which may well cause Thy sons to tremble. Is this, Great God, the army which Thou hast chosen for Thy defence? How great must our difficulties be, between two such foes! Remove far from us, O Lord, the temptation thus to give back scorn for scorn. All such emotions should be far from Thy priest. Whatsoever concerns souls should be serious in his eyes, even error itself, and his only weapons should be those of justice. It was thus Thy martyrs strove, thus the primitive apologists, who met the wildest, most atrocious calumnies with serious reasonings, solid arguments, and a patience worthy of Thy Cause. Never suffer us to say, "These men are unworthy to be shown the truth." No man here below is incurable, and all such proud thoughts must be displeasing to the Loving Heart of God. Let us rather arm ourselves against such contemptuous persecution with an upright life, with charity, with knowledge.

To meet contempt by irreproachable purity of life is at once to silence error and to win our adversary : it is simultaneously a work of apology and of charity. Men do not contend for long against him who does them good ; they are disarmed by those who tend their sick, teach their little ones, minister to their wants. Then again, we must bring our learning to bear upon the case; the early Christians met heathenish contempt by studding the crosses in their catacombs with jewels, and hanging lamps upon them. Old paintings have preserved the symbol of the faith thus adorned in the sight of human reason by the light of science and the brilliancy of genius. God does not despise this mode of winning respect; He has made great theologians, great philosophers, in order that human reason might be brought to a reckoning with them. This is a lesson to all. Let us work, then ; let us meet obscure contempt by a liberal diffusion of light. Light will always end by triumphing over darkness.

Moreover, in the season of contempt and persecution, let us redouble our faithfulness to the Church ;

let us put away every shadow of hesitation, or temptation to false shame—*non erubesco Evangelium ;* let us be doubly faithful to our persecuted King, more full than ever of respect for His priests. Who will esteem us, if we do not esteem ourselves? who will respect us, if we do not respect our brethren of the sanctuary? Let us be untiring in charity, consideration, reverence for God's priests. No officer will endure to hear an imputation cast upon the courage of one of his comrades ; why should a priest readily tolerate a suspicion, a calumny, a malicious jest at a brother's expense? Far be it from us to be thus cowardly. If men's reverence for one priest is lessened, it will be lessened for all ; and as men's reverence for the Priesthood dwindles away, so will their reverence for God diminish. And if persecution goes farther, and becomes violent ; if pursuit, blows, prison, exile, shedding of blood follow, then our duties, and with these our precautions and our means of defence, will change. Lord, how shall we make ready for such assaults?

First of all by detachment. " Beati pauperes spiritu." Blessed are they who possess as though they possessed not, and who use this world as not abusing it ! We must train our minds to lay aside all that is acceptable to the senses. All such things may be swept away in one hour's conflagration, and we must be prepared to exercise our functions in a garret or a cellar. We should frequently weigh over our own superfluities, and offer them mentally, so as not to be overcome or aggrieved when they are actually taken from us.

Next we require self-denial, in the shape of bodily mortification. That body which is accustomed to endure hardness, to suffer for the love of Jesus Christ, to bear the scourge of penitence, will be less aghast under the rude grasp of *gendarmes*, or under the rude pressure of a mob. It will be less likely to give way under trial, and add to the soul's perplexities.

And if the hour of actual danger comes, we must strive fully to enter into the spirit of apostolic faith; we must go straight back to the spirit of the catacombs; accept death, but not capitulate with conscience. We must not indulge in imprudences; the Church permits, even enjoins flight, although certain heresies have condemned it. But when prudence can do no more, when all is lost, then we must not temporise, we must fear nothing. Our words must be clear, strong, and firm. We must not be content to accept death with resignation, though that requires a composure which it may be hard to attain; we must rather encounter it with enthusiastic delight, even as in 1793 the maiden who could scarce have resigned herself coldly to death sprang joyfully up the scaffold to the tones of the *Salve Regina:* this is accordant with the Christian mind, and our national character.

And amid such days of trial, we must counterbalance our own weakness and want with an unlimited trust in God's help, knowing that He answers for us, acts for us, suffers and dies with us.

The Church does not fear a bloody persecution; she triumphs therein. But does that mean that we should wish for it? Far otherwise. The best general, he who is most confident of victory, is not free from sadness on the eve of a great battle. Persecution is a great evil for him who persecutes, and it leaves wounds in the heart of a nation which take more centuries to heal than they took days to inflict. The Church of England was smitten with such wounds, and her present life is more like a miraculous wakening from death than any mere healing. Let us then not be among those who cry out for persecution; let us beware of lightly invoking such grievous suffering upon our Mother the Church and our fellow men. On the contrary, let us labour for peace to the end, even against hope. Our strength for the battle will be greater, our victory more glorious, if we have done everything in our power to avert war. But, O Lord, if all our efforts to lead our age back to Thee are vain; if we are driven once more to minister the sacraments in secret places, we will call to mind the Church of France in 1793, the priests of the Catacombs, the Apostles, and He Who said, " Blessed

M

are ye, when men shall revile you, and persecute you, and shall say all manner of evil against you falsely for My Sake; rejoice and be exceeding glad, for great is your reward in Heaven!"

III.

Love of Man.

"Strike boldly at error, but let your heart be tender as a mother's towards men."[1] These words, worthy of Thyself, O Lord, were said to me a few days since by Thy holy Pontiff Pio Nono, and I would fain ponder them deeply.

God forbid, O Christ, that threats of persecution should diminish the love of man in the hearts of Thy priests! That priest who becomes the people's enemy, because they are betrayed into opposition and hatred, is unworthy of Thy Cross, incapable of maintaining thy cause in the world. Truly here we find our example in Thee, O Incarnate Word, for Thou wert ever misunderstood, despised, slandered, betrayed, persecuted, and yet Thou didst never cease to love men; Thy love reached even unto death! Thy love towards men was ever twofold; contending against their errors, full of tenderness towards

---

[1] "Blessez courageusement les erreurs, mais ayez un cœur de mère pour les hommes."

themselves ; and such should be the heart of a priest. We must strike boldly at error, prejudice, falsehood, inveterate calumnies perpetually renewed and ever flourishing ; we must abhor all evil, vice, injustice, oppression of the weak by the strong, triumph of insolence over right ; we must scourge impurity, the rich man who persecutes the poor, all that is dishonourable, however successful ; we must seek to develop everywhere, especially among our young men, a disgust for the common greed and abuse of money ; in short, we must strike, and strike boldly, at the passions of our age.

But we must love men, be indulgent to them, beware of discouraging them, never despise even the most contemptible among them. We may burn with righteous indignation—that is often a virtue ; but we must never be contemptuous. Indignation strikes in order to heal, contempt withers and kills ; we must possess an infinite fund of charity towards those whose errors are held in good faith, a boundless pity in leading them to truth ; unlimited consideration for all their objections and complaints ; unconquerable patience in quieting them ; we must meet all such erring souls with good and solid reasoning, we must win them by gentleness, "a soft answer turneth away wrath ;" in a word, we must make men feel beyond all doubt that we love them ; we must be "tender as a mother" towards them. A mother lives

in her children; it is she that has borne them, her
blood flows in their veins, her interests are inseparable
from theirs.   She rejoices in their joy, she suffers in
their woe, she blushes for their faults, she feels responsible for their shame or their glory.   Even so it
is with the priest; this is the true "cure of souls."
" Quis infirmatur et ego non infirmor?   Qui scan-
dalizatur et ego non uror?"   A celebrated woman
once wrote to her daughter, " *Ma fille, j'ai mal à
votre poitrine;*" and even so the priest must be able
to say to the sinner, " My son, I suffer in your soul."
What a well-spring of griefs, anxieties, and bitter
cares ! but they are the torments of love, and who
would dare to prefer the absence of love ? Yes, dear
Lord, may we feel the sharp pricks of that love and of
that zeal which consumed Thine Apostle ; we accept
all the consequences. Far be from us, Lord, the spirit
of indifference, that odious spirit of which Bossuet
says that it is the very mind of Cain when he said,
" Am I my brother's keeper?"   Each and every one
of us, we are the keepers of all our brethren.   One of
old said, " I am a man, and nothing human is a
stranger to me ;" and we say, " I am a priest; nothing
divine or human is a stranger to me."   Such is the
mind of the Gospel and of the Priesthood. But, Lord,
how am I to practise this zeal and this ardent
love ? The weakness of my soul as of my health

forbids me to aim at powerful preaching, or other great works. Guide me to humbler labours which may satisfy my longings and comfort me in my weakness.

i. And first of all, I must despise health where souls are in question. Sœur Rosalie, as she toiled on through her last illness, used to say to the young Sisters who strove to hinder her, "My children, let the doctors mind their business, and we will mind ours."[1] S. Carlo Borromeo used to say that a parish priest should not take to his bed until after his third attack of fever. Do men of the world give in so quickly, when weighty interests are at stake? Lawyers go into court in spite of illness; merchants are slow to quit their ledgers; soldiers follow the camp as long as they can sit a horse. Why, then, should a priest forsake the altar, the pulpit, or the confessional at the first touch of sickness? What toil, what watching we underwent in pursuit of earthly diplomas and degrees! and shall we claim the season of rest when Thou wouldst be served? *Absit !* I ask of Thee, then, courage to remain stedfast at my post through all minor hindrances.

ii. The pulpit will probably be forbidden to me, at all events for some time. If so, I must transfer

---

[1] " Laissons les médecins faire leur métier, et nous, faisons le nôtre."

preaching into the ordinary relations of life. I must study to use conversation for a good and serious end. Thou hast placed me in a world where much may be done by this means, but subject to certain conditions; above all, that of a solid faith—enlightened, but very simple and very sincere—a faith which cannot be disconcerted, which never concedes the unchangeable truth, but everywhere and always maintains its rights in their full integrity. This is more difficult than one would suppose under certain circumstances; nevertheless it is an indispensable condition of doing good. Then there is instruction : I must teach men to honour the faith, and be " ready to render an account of the hope that is in me." Charity sustains work, and the best of all intellectual charity is that which labours to impart a revered, well grounded, well maintained doctrine to men.

III. I must take refuge from men of the world and books with the poor and little children. I must strive to throw my whole heart into mission work among the poor. As for the children, Thou, Lord, hast made me see how great and real a good it is to catechise them. One's mind reverts thankfully to the substantial simplicity of fundamental truth, and one's heart seems to be purified by the contact of those young hearts which are so readily convinced by the light of Thy dogmas.

iv. Moreover, in extraordinary times one must lead an extraordinary life, and be prepared to follow the leading of God's Providence. One must be ready to be a nurse or hospital chaplain in seasons of epidemic; military chaplain in war, engineer in the face of fire; everybody's servant at sea; one must adapt oneself to circumstances with the utmost flexibility, and be ready to change all one's ways and habits on behalf of that love of God and men which can never change. The priest should be at home wherever there are souls to win.

Finally, Lord, from Thee Alone I can hope the gift of an earnest, generous heart, burning with love for the suffering, indulgent towards men, while inflexible towards sin and error; that priestly heart, in short, which none save Thou canst give. Oh! my God, direct the strong love, which I have perhaps hitherto misapplied, to the good of souls. Teach me true loving kindness. Amid all our anxiety for the future, it is a comforting thought that there are so many kindly hearts amid Thy priests; assuredly it will be these men that will save France and the Church. Grant me to be of the number, and teach me daily how Thy Love, as it fills my heart, can enlarge and expand it towards men.

We have seen Henri's ideal of death; this was his

ideal of life, and he was faithful to these inspirations, these promises, both in life and in death.

But before contemplating him in the presence of death, I have somewhat to say as to the weak point in his life, and the danger to which he exposed himself, a danger which cost him his life—that of the body—for his spiritual life remained intact, and went forth to find its full development in God. He had a special affection for the wise man's saying, "Surely in vain the net is spread in the sight of any bird."[1]

[1] Prov. i. 17.

CHAPTER VI.

IMPERFECTION.

AND now I am going to utter my complaint. I must express my heart's grief. Why was this noble creature, this *chef-d'œuvre de Dieu*, as he was well called by one of his best friends, to be so soon spent? Scarce come to maturity, not having yet attained the full command of his powers, and he was gone!

It is of Henri himself that I complain. I mourn that he is lost to us through his own fault. He sought death as much through a want of discipline as through impetuous courage, like a soldier who is killed when going beyond his post. In spite of all one's advice and entreaties, he fully illustrated that cruel dictum of science, "Men do not die, they kill themselves."[1]

I know Henri Perreyve's whole life, I know the entire history of his mind, body, and soul; and I affirm that he died a victim to that great evil which I can only call *priestly isolation*. Alone through the daily course of his life (as Père Lacordaire wrote to him

---

[1] "L'homme ne meurt pas, il se tue."

regretfully, " Alone, dear child, in your own room " [1]),
encountering alone the crowd which consumed him,
he did not know how to resist the forcible *entrainement*
of success, or the ceaseless interruptions of all those
who sought to sun themselves in his light, or draw
upon the stores of his zeal. Every day brought him
the work of ten priests. " Refuse all these applications, and keep to your own work," I used to urge.
" I am perpetually refusing," he would answer. In
fact he refused some six or seven out of every ten
applications, but even then there remained more
than he could accomplish. Besides his Professorship
of Moral Theology at the Sorbonne, which in itself
is enough to engross whoever fills it ; besides his
numerous writings, which would have been a sufficient
task, there was no end to his sermons, personal work
in every direction, endless correspondence, hearing
confessions, direction, *réunions* of young men, incessant visits, social intercourse without pause or limit !
And all this ate into his very life and fairly consumed
him.

About five years before his death Henri regained
a measure of strength, which, if wisely husbanded,
would have lasted for twenty years, but he poured it
forth in reckless waste ! I cannot describe my dis-
may when the day came on which I first perceived

[1] " Seul, mon enfant, dans un appartement à vous ! "

that he had evidently lost his powers of self-control,
that he was carried away. He had taken to evening
work, then to night work, to the sacrifice of his morn-
ings, to finding meditation an impossibility ; to the
doing away with all recollection. Even before things
came to this point, I used to write such notes as the
following to him :—

" MON ENFANT,—I cannot be silent. I feel it to
be my duty to warn you, to save your life, it may be.
We agreed some eight months ago, in accordance
with your physician's advice, that you were to take
entire rest for several years. You know that it is
Père Lacordaire's imperative opinion; you know how
urgently he spoke about it to me lately ; I am sure
he was not less urgent with you yourself. If you go
on as you are doing, in spite of all your friends, it
will become a really blameable infatuation. Be sure
that a relapse is not far off—it will probably come
within a few weeks ! Now forgive me ; it is my deep
affection which makes me speak. If you become
unfit for anything, or if we lose you before your time
through your own imprudence, it will be a sore wound
to us all." This note was signed by two Oratorians.

" This sort of thing cannot go on," Père Lacordaire said to me ; " he ought to have three years'
rest, not only for his body's sake, but for mind and
soul too. If he goes on with this active, broadcast

life he will break down, and moreover he will never
gain the strength, depth, and greatness which God
means him to have.   Let him come to me at Sorèze
for three years !"

Sorèze indeed !   Why forsooth did Lacordaire give
up his own life to the endless distractions of a
school, letting himself be ground to dust like corn
in a mill ?   Recollection does not depend upon a
man's geographical distance from Paris; it depends
upon the unity of his work, and the degree of his
own interior life.   It depends upon solitude with
God, *clauso ostio !*

Anyhow, all the efforts made by Henri's friends
were vain ; he was carried away and crushed.   "Oh,
what a profound horror I have in the depth of my
heart of his imprudence !" one of those who sorrows
piteously for his death writes to me ; and I say the
same.   It stirs my wrath to see the laws of life thus
neglected and trodden under foot, even by the best
of men.   This is no question of braving death in the
cause of duty.   When in 1864, Henri consented to
preach at Sainte Barbe to those young men whose
hearts his voice could reach better than any other, I
raised no opposition, although he was then well nigh
spent; and I could not but approve when he said, "I
refuse all work this year, but as to the Conferences at
Sainte Barbe, if I knew that I should die the day after

they are over, I should only undertake them the more resolutely. It is but what every subaltern does, when a dangerous post is allotted to him." But the "*Station de Sorbonne,*" which followed, was an unpardonable mistake and did really cost him his life, not many months later. By his own fault he deprived us of all that his mature life, his old age might have been. We have so few old or wise men ! and that chiefly because we are all more and more deficient in depth and recollection. The world moves on with ever increasing rapidity. Movement becomes multiplied and intensified in every shape, moral, intellectual, and physical. And beneath this surface movement, I fear, one discovers that there is a slackening of central impetus. We whirl about more, but we advance less.

I would fain dwell a few moments upon the evil which cost our dear young brother his life. I would warn others and myself against it, by analyzing it.

It is a universal blot ; every living thing finds the difficulty of self-recollection, of gathering itself together, and abiding stedfast at the heart's core. It is an evil incident alike to the flowers by the wayside, to all living bodies, to all hearts and minds. It is the *degenerare tamen* of Virgil, which, passing on from the grain of wheat, he applies to all nature. It is that which S. Bernard, with his deep insight has called " *evisceratio mentis,*" " the disembowelling

of the soul." S. Augustine alludes to the same evil,
under the same metaphor, "*viscera quædam animæ,*"
when he says that man throws the inner depths of his
soul into his outer life, "*projecit intima sua in via
sua.*" Life hurries on, spreads itself far and wide,
but the source of life dries up. What avails it to
conquer the world, if that conquest exhausts the life
within us? Yet this is the universal weakness of
all creation; it is the road which leads to death.
Let us consider the present time, and the tendency
of minds in this our day to rush forward. If we
are to believe one of the latest and ablest psychological authors, that mental and spiritual progress
consists in intensifying the inward life ;[1] in passing
(as mystic writers have well said) from that which
is without, to that which is within, and thence to that
which is highest ;—"*ab exterioribus ad interiora, ab
interioribus ad superiora,*"—if this, I say, be true,
surely at no time have the human mind and soul been
so utterly dispersed, plunged amid that which is external, which may perchance prove to be the "outer
darkness," of which we read in the Gospel. There
is a mighty central life within the vast sphere of a
man's soul, which seems to be forgotten, unheeded
by all ; a neglected sanctuary, a lost fountain head !
And owing to this, those who have wandered furthest

---

[1] "À remonter les degrés d'intériorité."

would fain assure us that no such invisible world has ever existed. These men tell us that our very soul's existence and that of God, and that science which teaches their union, the interior life, theology, metaphysics, are mere illusion. They end by denying the existence of the very source which gave them life.

In days of old there were monks whose whole life was absorbed in this great Centre, and who found peace, light, and happiness therein. To them it furnished the motive power, the life of all things. But in these days where shall we find such calm, deep minds, dwelling in the invisible, wrapt in heavenly things, ever facing eastwards amid the whirl of life? Who now believes in recollection, retirement, and prayer?

I have seen a discourse which, forty years ago, a learned magistrate ventured to produce, on the advantage of retirement for lawyers;[1] but, now-a-days, who would venture to proffer such an idea, who would give a moment's heed to it? Let it go! Enough, if we may presume to speak of the need for retirement in the priest's case! Yet a life of retirement and recollection, an interior life, a life of prayer, *de interna Christi conversatione*, of hidden communion with God; these are undoubtedly the greatest of all realities— realities which cannot pass away, an imperative need to

---

[1] " De l'utilité de la retraite pour l'avocat."

the soul. But, practically, these are all as empty words
to us. And this is the great danger of the world we
live in, in the actual state of men's minds. Who then
is there to resist this overwhelming danger, save the
priest? What is more essentially his office than the
duty of prayer and intercession for his people? And
what does that mean, save a fervent, effectual, ceaseless
effort to bring back that mass of minds and hearts,
ever so ready to disperse itself abroad, to the Father,
the Centre, to that sanctuary where He dwells, whence
He creates, inspires, renews all our being? *Pater qui
est in abscondito?* We know—I speak to my priestly
brethren—that all our strength lies in prayer and
faith, nourished in our souls by recollection and
retirement, by the habit of that interior life which
alone fosters holiness, light, and love. We shall never
become useful ministers of the Gospel by multiplying
our surface efforts, or by accumulating good works;
that can only be done through the mighty power of a
humble heart which leans on God, of a thoughtful
soul which drinks deep of Him. Therein, I say, lies
our strength to fulfil our duty, to save our people, and
to bring them back to God. And moreover, we know
well, there too abides the strength which upholds our
life,—the life of the soul, the mind, and the body,
ad tutamentum mentis et corporis. The soul without
recollection is as the body without sleep; fever must

come on, and death ensue. And if the soul be distracted, even through the very activity of its zeal, and
whatever may be the fruits of that zeal, it has not
used its powers as God willed it to do. A more
recollected labour would have borne better fruit, and
life would not have been consumed. This is the
reproach I bring against our dearly loved young
brother, Henri Perreyve—he was not self-possessed;
he did not know how to "possess his soul." If we
could but have kept to the primitive ideal! If we
could have spent our lives working together, a few
brethren, *omnes unanimiter in eodem loco;* in a daily,
real intercourse of thought and soul, upholding, re-
straining, kindling one another! Ah! then he would
yet be among us!

Henri began by adopting that organization of the
priestly life as idealized by S. Philip Neri and Cardinal
de Bérulle, but illness cut the trial short. Nor was
the experiment then imbued with that warm spring
life which would have fostered his work and his life.

"*Nec res hunc teneræ possent perferre laborem.*"

He found a far more severe labour in isolation; it
was all unbridled zeal, abuse of energy, distraction,
and thus finally his life was crushed out!

N

CHAPTER VII.

DEATH.

I.

AND now I come to Henri Perreyve's death.
Thank God, he died as he had lived, with the
same bold decision, the same yearning towards his
true aim—perfect beauty.

Launched as he was amid the most exciting labours,
the most noble successes of life, carried away in them
as he was, by an impetus he could no longer control,
nevertheless he stopped his fervid career, he turned
round and faced approaching death with simplicity,
resolution, and calmness.

But a few months before the end, he wrote, " I
have really overtried my strength during the past
year; I am really very tired. The doctors use big
words, which would frighten me if I clung closely
to life. But I do not cling to it, I can most honestly
say, and I am quite ready to accept the *point extrême.*
Unfortunately, before one is dead, one must die;[1]

---

[1] " Malheureusement, pour être mort il faut mourir."

and that is a serious and awful step, specially when taken deliberately. I comfort myself with the thought that, as I have done everything vigorously all through my life, perhaps *le bon Dieu* will leave me some power of exertion to the last !"

His wish was fulfilled, the illness made rapid progress, and he died with all his old energy about him. On the very day of his death, Henri's last act was a cry to God's Eternal Goodness : " Satiabor cum apparuerit Gloria Tua :"—" When I wake up in Thy Likeness I shall be satisfied with it." And the last words he uttered were in answer to an act of the love of God made for him, when he murmured, " Oh yes, I love Him with all my heart."

But let us pause here a moment ; let us seek to be absolutely real in all things, above all in such a matter as this. Do not let us imagine that to be the most beautiful death which is most free from all shrinking and terror. The disciple is not greater than his Lord. and Christ Himself, Who conquered death, has vouchsafed to reveal His own dying anguish to us. Three times He prayed, " My Father, if it be possible, let this cup pass from Me;" and amid His utter desolation on the Cross He cried out : " My God, my God, why hast Thou forsaken Me !"

It may be that those souls in which life is strongest feel the terror of death most keenly. None has ever felt it as Christ Jesus did. Those vigorous souls which are united to Him feel it like to and with Him, and leaning on His Cross, they triumph over death, passing in triumph to the other side of the gulf. No need then to marvel at what took place an hour before Henri died. " Towards seven o'clock," says the loving friend who watched over his last hours, " he made a sudden effort to raise himself in his bed ; his face was haggard and bathed in sweat, his lips colourless, but his kindling eyes sparkled, and were as though fixed with an expression of intense terror on some present though invisible enemy ; while twice he cried out, ' I am afraid ! I am afraid !'" [1]

Again, I say it, the disciple is not greater than his Lord, and this cry of anguish is but the echo of that voice from the Cross, " My God, my God, why hast Thou forsaken Me !" But even as after that great and bitter cry, the dying Son of God breathed forth the words, " Father, into Thy Hands I commend My Spirit," so the dying disciple, leaning on His Master's Guiding Hand, added, after his cry of terror, " It is not of God that I am afraid;" and then grace was given him that his last earthly words might be an act of love of God. " Oh yes ! I love Him with all my heart," he murmured, pressing his lips ardently to the Figure of his beloved Master.

[1] " J'ai peur ! j'ai peur!"

II.

Neither do I marvel at that other terror, which one may call *intellectual terror*, and which assaulted Henri Perreyve during his latter days, a trouble which we had discussed at length some months before. We were talking then about what between ourselves we called " the temptation of believing all or nothing" *(la tentation du tout ou rien)*. We had said that the greatest souls and most vigorous minds are sometimes forced by the natural order of things to grapple with absolute doubt: *all or nothing*—the most vigorous,—Descartes to wit,— are able forthwith to find the " all." But poor weak minds cannot find anything for themselves, and these either are never tried, or they wisely draw back, refusing to dally with temptation ; while if, on the other hand, a guilty weakness lets them be drawn under the fascinating spell, they run a risk of being blinded by the mere sight of darkness.[1] If that happens, their reason will be altogether upset, they will neither believe any more, nor understand any more. If, nevertheless, they affect to teach, their whole dogma will consist in a denial of reason, and they become real sophists. Sophists are those who have been defeated in their radical intellectual trial. Under any circum-

[1] " Weak eyes on darkness dare not gaze ;
It dazzles like the midday blaze."

stances, the first effect of great intellectual trial is,
and must be, a certain intellectual terror, which even
the greatest minds undergo ; the holiest souls are
sometimes called to bear it; it is enough to instance
S. Francis de Sales, S. Ignatius, S. Alfonso Liguori,
and S. Vincent de Paul.

" But," Henri said, " can you see of what practical
use such a temptation to deny everything can be ?"

" Yes, certainly.   It is God's lesson to teach us to
hold fast the groundwork of truth by our own personal effort and foresight, by our own free and
deliberate choice.   There is a striking mystery in this,
namely, that God so loves men that He wills to give
them that which at first seems impossible, somewhat
of an independent existence. [1]   God begins the work
in us, but He obliges us to finish it ourselves by
beginning the whole thing anew.   To this end, He
withdraws, and leaves the mind face to face with
a void blank.   Then the terrified soul cries out,
' My God, why hast Thou forsaken me ? '   ' *Pater, ut
quid dereliquisti me ? '*   And the Father answers, ' Rise
up of thyself, rise up and walk ;' ' *Surge et ambula.'*
That temptation to believe in nothing tells us that
there is no Christ, no future, no Father in Heaven, no
God, no soul, neither aim, law, truth, nor duty.   There
is nothing.   All that men call religion, reason, feel-

[1] " Quelque chose de *l'être par soi.*"

ing, conscience, poetry, and philosophy is a mere nothing."

" *Cher Père,*" Henri said, " how do you meet the question of absolute negation ? "

" Perhaps it would suffice to say that if the dilemma of all or nothing holds good, that in itself grants the ' *all ;* ' because as a fact THERE IS SOMETHING. Facts prove existence, to say nothing of right ; and nothingness is contradicted by facts as well as by right."

" It is obvious, and though subtle, the reasoning is solid."

" I think we may add this rule ; when the failing mind takes to dreaming thus, waken it and bid it attend. That spirit of evil slumber says there is naught ; well, then, open your eyes and see. What does exist ?

" The world exists, and I myself, and other men ; daylight, the starry heavens, the immensity of life. All this is positive and certain. So then to start with, there is something, and something beautiful too. But do you not see how much is involved by this something ? "

" I feel it, but I can feel better than I can reason."

" Naturally. But look again, look at the starry sky. To me, I own, that is always a substantial abiding *point d'appui.* I know, as though I could behold them, that this boundless space is peopled with thou-

sands of worlds like our own; and how that knowledge revives our old convictions! Imagine these
hosts of worlds, these celestial multitudes, living under
the same attraction and the same light with ourselves;
they have necessarily the same geometry, the same
logical axioms, the same moral axioms, I might venture to say the same religion. They love as we love,
and with a like heart; they invoke the same Father,
and ask the same blessings of Him. Moreover, were
ours the only humanity in creation, this reasoning
would be the same. The millions and millions of men
who have succeeded and will succeed each other to
the end would suffice for this. Or were there but
one man in creation, surely that would be enough.
Intelligent and free, must he not attain to whatever is
involved by intelligence and liberty? This much
then is clear; namely, that we are an immense
assembly of free intelligent minds, seeking one and
the same thing; an enduring life, ever growing in
eternal love. And this it is of which the universe is
composed.

"But what would you think of those who, standing
face to face with this fact, the fact of the universe and
its motion, should say: 'All this comes to nothing; all
men seek and will seek for ever, but will find naught?'"

"I think, as you often say, that such minds are im-
perfect, mutilated."

" Exactly so ; reason tells us that he who seeks finds. Therefore we shall find ; we shall find all things, the Father, our celestial brethren, eternal life. Everything has been told us, demonstrated to us. The commonest effort of reason, from the world's point of view, gives us ' all ' from the first ; and the mind which cannot see this is deficient in reasoning power. Remember what I say ;—He is deficient in reasoning power who cannot work out for himself, or grasp when put before him, that simple argument addressed to all hearts and minds, which has been eternally sanctified and glorified by Christ's own gracious illustration. ' If your son ask bread, which of you will give him a stone ? ' the Lord asked ; ' How much rather will your Heavenly Father give good things to them that ask Him ? ' The depth and power of this sublime and popular reasoning will be appreciated when the science of logic, now extinguished among us, lives again. Yes, thanks be to God, we possess a simple religion, and the slightest effort of reason, when brought to bear upon the argument of ' all or nothing,' proves the ' all.' The ground will not give way beneath our faith."

Such was our last philosophical conversation, some few months before Henri Perreyve's death. It enables me to understand what he meant when during the weariness of his last days he prayed so

continually, " Lord increase our faith ! "   And when
he added, " Now is the time when I thank God for
giving me a simple religion," he meant, " When my
mind fails and seems for a moment to fall into the
slumber of general doubt, the slightest philosophical
effort, the old natural mode of reasoning, hinders me
from going further, and brings me safely back, for
it restores God, the foundation of ALL, to me.   The
smallest visible resting point holds all together,
confirms all, and re-kindles life and religion in
my heart."   How much more must such thoughts
have filled his mind when, following out the prayer,
" Lord, increase our faith," he asked that friend
of his childhood who was as the guardian angel of
his last hours to read those soul-stirring words of
S. Paul, the eighth chapter of his Epistle to the
Romans : " I am persuaded that neither death, nor
life, nor angels, nor principalities, nor powers, nor
things present, nor things to come shall be able to
separate us from the love of God, which is in Christ
Jesus our Lord ! "

" Every word filled our hearts more and more
deeply," says the Abbé Bernard. " Jesus Christ was
with us as with the disciples at Emmaus, and our
hearts burned within us as He talked with us. I could
scarce go on with the sacred words, and Henri was
crying quietly and silently. As I read the concluding

words, 'I am persuaded that neither death, nor life, nor any other creature shall be able to separate us from the love of God,' we both broke down, and tears became sobs. Soon Henri squeezed my hand and said, 'Oh ! leave me alone with God, *à demain.*' I was going away, full of awe, when he exclaimed, ' Or rather give me the Holy Communion.' I went quickly to fetch the Blessed Sacrament, gave It to him, and then, without breaking the deep, sacred silence by a word, I left him peacefully making his act of Thanksgiving, inwardly asking God, if it might be so, to take my dear friend to be with Himself that very night."

III.

But I must go back to the time when, a few weeks earlier, Henri began to feel the approach of death. Being told of a powerful union of intercessory prayer for him, he said, "All the week I have been pondering about death, and I have accepted it without regret or fear. Indeed, the whole time I have heard a *responsum mortis* within. I am very grateful for the prayers offered on my behalf, but I do not ask life. It would be impossible for me to pray for it."

It is one thing inwardly to feel the approach of death, but quite another to be told of it by those around. After the first solemn announcement, he

asked for the Holy Viaticum. Utterly worn out as
he was with illness, he would get up, and put on his
cassock, as though preparing to celebrate. He went
to the room where the altar was prepared. At that
very moment I arrived, and learnt, almost simultaneously with Henri, the imminence of his danger. That
was the last time I saw him up ; he had known for
the last hour that his life was nearly spent. I can see
him yet, full of energy and sweetness as usual, saying
with his wonted smile, " I am quite at peace, *mon bon
Père*, quite happy." By God's grace I shall never
forget that picture ; his noble bearing, the cassock
he was so proud to wear, his marble-white face, his
large black eyes, his loving, large-hearted glance, and
those last words, " *bien en paix.*" Yes, indeed, my
dearly loved child, we shall meet again, I trust, in that
peace which passeth not away !

From that moment he kept his face stedfastly
turned towards death, in peaceful recollection. Just
now I blamed him for allowing his life to be distracted
by excessive activity and a consuming multiplicity of
work ; but henceforth, so far from clinging to the
many who loved him so devotedly, he sought silence
above all things, asking to be left by himself, and
remaining alone for hours. It was the same with
Lacordaire ; during his last days he was unwilling to
be interrupted in his solitude with God. His disciple

experienced a like divine attraction. He was now
meditating on the other side of death, the bright,
immortal side, which comes after darkness and pain.
" I see now," he said to Père Charles Perraud, " how
good it is to have accustomed myself to think of death
as a welcome, kindly friend. What a blessing it is
to be a Christian ! I never felt it so much before.
You must preach it all your life !" And going on still
further in submission to God's Will, he attained that
highest and most desired point, the greatest act of
which man's will is capable, that of saying, in spirit
and truth, with his Master in the garden of Geth-
semane, " Father, not my will, but Thine be done."

Loving God's Will, not in word only, or in mere
thought, but in full truth,—knowing God to be on the
other side of death, therefore choosing to die, asking
earnestly for the moment when that awful gulf might
be passed ; such was the grace so abundantly poured
out upon him.

All who knew him know well that he never uttered
any merely conventional words. Whatever Henri said
was true ; was what he had seen and felt. But to appreciate his words concerning death one must remember
what he knew, believed, and felt. A living man can,
and ought to say, " I have life, and I will keep it."
We have the germ of endless life ; and death, like birth,
is the starting point of a new and rapid development,

an indispensable transformation like those living organisms which are so marvellously metamorphosed before our eyes. We carry each one within us a hidden treasure of powers, which surge and eddy here, but will find their vent elsewhere. It is this hidden treasure which death reveals. One often sees souls who are keenly alive to these wonders as death approaches, and in all sober truth, without any delusion, such souls prefer death to life ; and that not in virtue of any theological or philosophical process of reasoning, but in verity and truth.

That was a most real feeling which our dear Henri expressed, when, an hour after his friend had told him that his life was nearly ended, he said, " You cannot think how happy I have been since you told me that I am really dying." And as the actual moment was delayed, he said, " I never was more disappointed than during these few days, to find that I could not die."

So again, when for a brief moment he thought he was returning to life, Henri said, " I am sorry for it. I have grown used to the thought of death ; I lived with it, and was happy in it ; and this is a harder sacrifice. I shall have to accept a wretched, weary life. What a useless, miserable creature I shall be for ever so long ! I would rather have died : but God's Will be done in life as in death."

And when at length he was told in reply to his own distinct urgent inquiry, that death was close at hand, his answer was, " I understand ; thank you. Then it will be to-day? I must make ready for the great struggle ; you must give me the Holy Viaticum." And he received the Holy Communion with intense fervour and peace. But these last details must be told by the Abbé Bernard himself.

He died that same day.

Ten days before his death, Henri wrote the following lines.

" IN THE NAME OF THE FATHER, OF THE SON, AND OF THE HOLY GHOST.

" I die in the faith of the Catholic Church, to whose service I have had the blessing of dedicating my life since I was twelve years old.

" I bless my relations and friends tenderly.

" I intreat all who remember me to pray long for my soul, that God, turning away His Eyes from my sins, may vouchsafe to receive me into Eternal Rest and Peace. I hope for this through the Merits of our Lord Jesus Christ. Amen.

" Once more I bless all who are dear to me —my parents, benefactors, teachers, my fathers and brethren in the priesthood, my spiritual children, all the dear young fellows who have loved me, all those souls to which I have been bound on earth

by the bonds of a common faith and love in Jesus
Christ.

"PAX VOBIS."[1]

IV.

And now, SURSUM CORDA! Thanks be to God,
he died in charity, he died in love. His last words
having been to bless his relations and friends, and
his will being finished, he adds as it were a codicil,
to repeat this benediction. "Once more I bless all
who are dear to me . . . all those souls to which I
have been bound on earth," and he goes on to say,
"by the bonds of a common faith and love in Jesus
Christ," meaning clearly to distinguish between such
sacred ties and those heedless souls which were con-

---

[1] "Au nom du Père, du Fils, et du Saint Esprit.

"Je meurs dans la foi de l'Église Catholique, au service de
laquelle, depuis l'âge de douze ans, j'ai eu le bonheur de con-
sacrer ma vie.

"Je bénis tendrement mes parents et mes amis.

"Je conjure tous ceux qui garderont quelque souvenir de moi
de prier longtemps pour le salut de mon âme, afin que Dieu,
détournant ses regards de mes péchés, daigne me recevoir dans
le lieu du repos et du bonheur éternel.

"J'espère cette grâce par les mérites de Notre Seigneur Jésus
Christ. Amen.

"Je bénis encore une fois tous ceux qui me sont chers, mes
parents, mes bienfaiteurs, mes maîtres, mes pères et mes frères
dans le sacerdoce, mes fils spirituels, tant de chers jeunes gens
qui m'ont aimé, toutes les âmes auxquelles j'ai été uni sur la terre
par le lien d'une même foi, et d'un même amour en Jésus Christ."

tinually seeking him, merely with a view to sun themselves for a passing moment in the light of his grace
and eloquence. But still I know he did give his
blessing to all such immortal souls, and asked that
they might win depth and a real love of God. It never
occurred to Henri to say that he forgave his enemies;
first because if a priest has any such, it is scarce
needful that he should announce his fulfilment of so
simple a duty; and, moreover, Henri did not know
of any to forgive! Who indeed did not love him?
To whom did he ever give offence? Where were his
enemies? I cannot suppose that such ever existed!
I know of one eminent man who, differing from him
in opinion, was once harsh and unjust to Henri in
public. But I would that I might here record the
noble, Christian-like, full and perfect reparation
offered by that good man; so that in truth I must
take both fault and reparation as a fresh proof how
all were constrained to love Henri. Indeed, I believe that if we find but little love on earth, it is
not so much because the hearts of men refuse to love
their brethren, as that the greater part of mankind
refuse to deserve love. For the most part, hearts
are ready to own allegiance to all that is good and
beautiful, to all that has a right claim to their love;
Henri had that claim set forth in his glorious moral
beauty, and all his life he experienced the result.

From childhood he met with kindness and goodwill
on all sides ; his whole life was like the short, bright
journey which, when twenty, he made alone across
the Pyrenees, and which he describes in a letter from
Spain.   After narrating the endless unexpected kindness and hospitality which he had encountered, he says,
" Is it not just like a dream, or a story out of the
Arabian Nights ?   Really, after having done it all, I
cannot hardly believe it myself !   If all my relations
and friends had been stationed along the road to
Spain, I could not have been more affectionately or
generously received.   I suppose *le bon Dieu* meant to
teach me a great lesson of love to man, and I hope
I shall not forget it."

His whole life was like this.   Friendship, kindness, affection, deep enthusiastic regard, holy and
noble love met him at every turn throughout his
course.   First there was the gentle pious boy, Eugène
Bernard, his friend and confidant from the days of
their joint preparation for First Communion to Henri's
death-bed, when we find him at once priest and friend,
confessor, almost Sister of Charity; and then the large-
hearted Charles Perraud, "*mon Charles!*" so entirely
one with Henri in mind and aim, in courage, intelligence, goodness ; who throughout his brief career
was his sworn brother at arms and true comrade !

Then again his meeting with M. Biot, who at once

was fascinated by him. Then Frédéric Ozanam
moulding his boyhood, and Lacordaire inspiring his
youth, writing to him, "You dwell for ever in my
heart, as a son and a friend." Next we find him
among the young vigorous hearts of the newly restored Oratory, amid whose fervid warmth he passed
the springtime of his vocation. Forcibly constrained to quit this resting-place by ill-health, wherever he was sent by medical advice he always found
friends disputing who should do most for him. He
discovered how far hospitality can go in that friendly
family where he met Ampère, who at once took the
young priest to his heart. M. Cousin, who will
scarcely be suspected of weakness, but who has a
feeling heart, said of Henri to me, " I have seen an
angel !"

What shall I say of the way he was received by
his superiors in the priesthood, of the unusual privi-
leges offered to him on all sides, favours which he
generally rejected on behalf of other men, who have
themselves told me of such facts ; or of the affection
he met with, in spite of the times, amid the noble,
pious group of catechists at Saint Thomas d'Aquin?
of the reception, the love he met with at the Lycée
Saint Louis, and later at Saint Barbe, from pupils of
every age, and from all the masters ; "all the dear
young fellows who have loved me"? Summoned to the

Sorbonne, to say nothing of our excellent colleagues, Henri found in the beloved and venerable Dean, not merely fatherly kindness, but hearty affection, that watchfulness which followed his every step, removing hindrances, and counteracting weariness, an affection which has not ended with the grave, but which demands the very tribute I am now writing. Then again the feeling experienced for him by that great, noble-hearted man Montalembert, who in return received no small share of comfort from Henri's powers of consolation ; and the solid, abiding hearty friendship of Augustin Cochin, of whom he once said to me, expressing therein my own thoughts, " People do not know him yet ; some day they will realize what he is!"

May Henri's last blessing fall abundantly on all these, and on the many more whom I know but may not name, as also on those yet unknown !

V.

And now yet once again, " Sursum corda !" Let us apply to Henri his own words over the tomb of his friend Herman de Jouffroi : " He who dies, after such a life, in that grace which makes saints, his lips pressed to the Saviour's Cross, goes from our earthly dwellings straight to God's Own Heart. How shall we pity him ? how pity ourselves ? Now he sees and knows. That eager intellect, that vigorous will, that

deep, generous heart, all are filled and satisfied ; and
yet you are not comforted, ye who loved him ! You
ask if all is over between you? You think it hard that
a man should reach the first steps of his career, and
just as he enters upon it, full of vigour, strength, and
noble aims, all should at once be snatched from his
grasp—all his work, his struggles frustrated. But oh !
my friends, are you certain that death truly does this?
Are you so certain that our happy brethren's labours
are rudely frustrated, and that they can no longer
promote those great objects for which they toiled?
Rather is it not true that 'living and moving in God,'
the eternal dwelling-place of souls, they may yet act
invisibly upon this world, and, through their uplifted
inspirations, bring about great results? Is it not true,
as has been well said, that even in this world 'the
dead have more life than we'?"

Such was his belief, such his hope.

During his last days, Henri said to Père Adolphe
Perraud (the same friend to whom aforetime he wrote,
" Courage, happy friend ; you carry all our vocations
bound up with your own !"), " *Cher ami*, I wanted to
see you to say good-bye. We shall not cease to work
together for God and His Church, shall we? Adieu !
I am so perfectly happy ;—Give me your blessing."

Yes indeed, this is what we need to realize and
believe more fully, that the dead are with us yet. But

for the most part men will not think of the dead, or
dwell with them ; grovelling in that which is visible,
they live in a dull forgetfulness of those they have
ceased to behold.   Happy they who cling to the
invisible, who cherish and live in the memory of those
whom they no longer see !   May we but be worthy to
feel their nearness in our hearts !

Men feel that all cannot be at an end between
us and those who have passed out of sight, and
hence the childish inventions of spirit-rapping and
the like.   But there is something better than this :
our links to the spiritual world though unseen are
powerful, and our longings, our hopes of communion
with the departed, will never cease.   Surely it is time
for Christians to be more faithful in this matter to
their belief ; for those thinkers who deserve the name
to give a deeper attention to this great question.

As a real *savant* said to me not long since, " If
men would but give, for one century, the same amount
of effort, time, and labour to the moral sciences and
study of the soul, which for the two last centuries they
have bestowed upon the physical and natural sciences
and mathematics, what marvellous and unforeseen
results might be obtained !   If men did but perceive
ever so faintly, concerning the soul, that which science
is beginning to discover as to the astronomical constitution of the universe, namely, that it is a vas

invisible, central world, taking a visible shape in some of its results, which sooner or later will solve many an enigma! And were we less superficial in our meditations, we might obtain some insight as to what is to be found in the depths of the soul, in those vast invisible depths, which we too studiously shun, into which we too often refuse even to cast a glance."

The farther natural science advances, the more richness, beauty, harmony, the more wondrous results, worthy of God's Hand, it discovers in the visible world ; and surely there would be a like result in spiritual science. They who seek to explore its depths will assuredly find that those mental regions with which we are familiar are shallow waters as compared therewith ; and it will tell us further that in the midst of those depths, in the very centre, so to say, a sanctuary will be found, and in that sanctuary God's throne, and that there it is that the souls of men meet and are united in their common Centre—God.

Thanks be to God for our glorious possession of the Catholic Faith, which teaches us the Communion of Saints, which gives us the help of their intercession and fellowship, which sets before us the union of the Church triumphant and the Church militant, and the mutual co-operation of both to bring the whole world within Christ's Kingdom !

Would that all men, whatsoever they be, would

ponder this truth. The mighty Church of Christ professes this as an article of faith; it is Christ's own teaching. Is it not, moreover, an universal and essential article of faith in every religion, every heart, and mind, even among those heathen savages who believe that the souls of their departed ancestors return to dwell in their sons and augment their daring?

S. Paul said, "I have you in my heart." "*Eo quod habeam vos in corde.*" Accept the truth of this expression of holy love; it may be profaned, but nothing can destroy its fundamental truth. Christ Himself, before withdrawing His visible Presence from us, declared, "Lo, I am with you alway, even to the end of the world": "*Ecce ego vobiscum sum omnibus diebus, usque ad consummationem sæculi.*"

Happy they to whom it is given to accept the true Catholic Faith, in all its life and fulness! They carry heaven about within them. God is in them, and Jesus Christ, and the souls of the blessed who rest in Him, are already their friends and companions. Our dear young brother possessed this real stedfast faith, and his whole life bore its stamp. He shall speak for himself as to his belief in that communion with the blessed dead who rest in the Lord.[1]

[1] Frédéric Ozanam entirely shared this belief. On the occasion of his mother's death he wrote :

LYON, *Noël*, 1839.—"No struggle, no agony, naught save a sleep, through which she retained almost a smile, a faint,

"My fellowship with Frédéric Ozanam did not end with his death; rather I may say that in its deepest, most direct form, that which has had the most powerful influence over my life, it only began after his death. It has been said that the dead have a more real life than ours; and perhaps we gain more

gradually failing breath,—and then there came a moment when that stopped, and we were orphaned. How can I describe the desolation, the tears which burst forth, and nevertheless the inexpressible, inexplicable inward peace we felt,—the sensation as though some great new blessing had come upon us, which came over not us only, but other near and dear members of our family." (Lettres, I. 57.) And again :

PARIS, *Jan.* 31, 1841.—" At first all consolation seems impossible, almost unwelcome to one's grief. I have known that mood, but it did not last. Soon another stage came in which I began to feel that I was not alone; an indescribable sweetness entered into the depth of my heart, it seemed a sort of assurance that I was not forsaken. It was a sense of loving, though invisible companionship; it was as though a cherished soul overshadowed me with its wings. And just as formerly I knew my mother's step or heard her voice, so now when a cheering thought rekindled my strength, or a good desire moved my mind, or a healthy impulse confirmed my will, I could not help believing that it was still her doing. And now, at the end of two years, when there has been time to clear away all that might belong to the first lively impressions of sorrow, I feel the like. There are times when I am suddenly drawn, as though she were there, at my side, above all when I need it most there are hours of tender intercourse between mother and son, hours when I weep more perhaps than I did in the first days of my loss; but my sadness is mingled with an ineffable joy. When I have been doing good, when I have been ministering to the poor she loved

from the living souls set free, than from those who yet live amongst us.   In my own case I cannot doubt it, so much I gained from that precious soul of which I speak, after it had departed to our God.   Towards the end of our vacation in 1853, when I came to Paris to enter upon the ecclesiastical life, to leave my father's house for that of God, I sorely needed in so anxious a season some strong hand to help me in cutting myself loose from the world, and in raising me to another world of thought, a new life.   This hand was stretched out to me from the grave.

"The first time that I saw Ozanam's coffin, it was in a subterranean chapel of Saint Sulpice.   In that chapel I had spent the best hours of my childhood; it was there that during three years I was prepared for my first Communion; it was there that I made my first promise to be God's servant for ever.   I had never been within the sacred walls since that time, and now at the end of ten years, when on the eve of fulfilling

so well, when I am at peace with the God she served so truly, I feel that she smiles upon me.   Sometimes when praying, I seem to hear her voice joined to mine, as we used to pray every evening before the crucifix.   And often (I may say it to you, though I could not tell it to others) when I have the blessing of Holy Communion, when the Saviour vouchsafes to visit me, I feel as though she followed Him to my poor heart as she used so often to follow Him when carried to the homes of the poor as their Viaticum, and at such times I have a very firm belief in her presence with me."   Vol. II. letter 3.

that promise, I returned thither, I was led there to receive a sterner, more mature lesson, that of death, beside the bier of a teacher and a friend. For long I prayed and meditated there. A few days later the coffin was removed to the Carmes, and placed in a vault beneath that church, in the chapel of the souls in purgatory. I frequently went thither; my dear friend's widow, who was now left alone in this world, used sometimes to trust the flowers she could not herself carry to his resting-place to me; I used to take them thither in her stead, and the thoughts of self-renunciation, of casting aside the world, of entire devotion to God, which absorbed me at that time, invested that coffin with an indescribable, invincible fascination for me, such as I scarcely venture to acknowledge.

" I used to enter the door of that vault as I might have entered the room of a friend in fulfilment of a welcome appointment. To put down the light, to arrange the flowers, to wipe away the damp which hung about the coffin, these were my first offices; and then kneeling down, my head resting on that venerated wood, I used to remain as one spell-bound. My heart leapt within me with strange bursts of joy and freedom ; I felt ready to die for God, to serve the cause of truth, of Christianity, of justice. I was willing to die to a life of pleasure, even to the memory of the past. I laid myself, as it were, in that coffin.

I entered into the Gospel words, ' Except a corn of wheat fall into the ground and die, it abideth alone.' Kneeling there, I threw my arms around my friend's coffin, I pressed my lips to it ; I loved to inhale the peculiar scent of the damp wood with a wild delight at which I cannot but wonder now. I used to feel as though I were embracing the Cross of Jesus, that Cross to which He was about to bind me, and which I grasped with an energy of love I have scarcely tasted since. They were wondrous hours which I spent thus.

" So far from exaggerating all this now, it is far less deep and vivid than it was, and I am altogether incapable of expressing it as I fain would do. With a heart strengthened by such impressions, and upheld by this strong hand which seemed to be reaching out to me from another world, I was able to pass, without any great shrinking, from the secular to the religious life. Of a truth I soon relapsed into weakness, for as soon as God's Arm is withdrawn how can one do aught but totter and fall ? The first trial of my strength was a continued mortal depression, which alarmed me the more that it was so contrary to my natural temperament. But my Dear Lord did not leave me comfortless, and once more He made use of that friendly hand to strengthen me. That hand gave me fresh courage by pointing out the hollowness of all short-lived earthly things ; the true dignity of real sacrifice, the fruitfulness of works done for God alone, the power of a soul chosen of God. All this I learnt from Frédéric Ozanam.

" For all this, ill expressed as it here is, but ordained from childhood for the good of my soul, may the Lord Jesus, my Master, be blessed !"

· And I too, for my part, as I close this labour of love, I would say, " For all this, ill expressed as it is in this book, but which concerns the life of God in the soul, may the Lord Jesus, our Master, be blessed !"

Moreover, dear son in the faith, that which you looked for from your blessed dead, we in our turn await from you. On your deathbed you promised, " We shall not cease to work together ;" and of a truth I believe that you do work with us. Adolphe Perraud, to whom you spoke those words, is now your successor, and it may be that, unseen, you sustain him in his nobly fulfilled task. Two great boons, which I may not name here, you have already won for those you love. And how often, amid care and sorrow, I have said within myself, " Whence this kindling of heart ? this sunshine which so reminds me of him ?—the very brightness and warmth which he ever seemed to carry with him ? Why should it not yet be himself who brings it ?"

Oh, my friends ! let us strive by prayer, by recollection, by the true life in the depths of our soul, to learn, while we are yet together in this world, how to live with those who are in Heaven !

And ye dear ones, who have gone before us, all ye whom we have known and loved, whom we love yet, abide with us ! Succour us with your co-operation, with your Christ-like heart, your glorified spirit ! Ye too, unknown guardians, followers of Jesus Christ, holy workers for God ; ye saintly ones who, in your tender womanhood, have trodden in the steps of His Blessed Mother, comfort us in our present sadness, be at our side in the toil which will lighten our earthly darkness, as it brings us nearer truth and love, nearer Heaven itself! Comfort us in that death hour, which ever draws nearer, if it may be, by some conscious indication of the friendly band of living and loving souls which await each one of us with a joyous welcome on the other side of Jordan !

O my God, give us grace to believe that Thou art ever present within our souls ; that Thy Throne is in our hearts. Give us grace to believe, O Incarnate Lord Jesus, that Thou art indeed with us, now and always, to the end of the world ; and that by faith and love we may safely rest our weariness on Thy Breast. Give us grace to believe in that holy company of glorified saints, more numerous, brighter far than sun and stars, which surges, like a sea of

light, around Thy Throne, O Father, around Thy
Heart, O Dear Jesus ; and teach us that where Thou
art, even in our hearts, they are with Thee !

O Christ, teach us to live ; teach us to die. Give
us grace to grasp Thy wondrous law, "Whoso liveth
and believeth in me shall never die." "*Qui vivit et
credit in me, non morietur in æternum.*" (John xi. 26.)

Brethren beloved in the Lord, we will keep this
word ; we will not die ! Cleaving to God, upheld by
those immortal living souls which are in God and
therefore with us, let us learn to say, in spirit and
in truth, "We live, and we will live."

Freed from that fear of death which makes man
a mere slave, let us toil on, and strive to lead the
world to fulfil its end. Possessed of eternal life, let
us venture upon labours which men call impossible ;
let us arm ourselves with invincible boldness. Let us
fearlessly and resolutely undertake to educate mankind ; let us pour a tenfold larger force of husbandmen into the harvest field of the Lord. Let us
become God's workmen. A great Bishop has said
that, to be worthy of this work, men must either
be born great, or become great.[1] Well ! let us

---

[1] "Pour porter le caractère sacerdotal, c'est-à-dire pour se
dévouer tous les jours de sa vie, *il faut être né grand ou le devenir ;*
des cœurs vulgaires, des caractères faibles, des esprits abattus, une
éducation commune n'y suffiraient pas ; aujourd'hui surtout, les

become great through humility, through winning to
ourselves the great minds of our noble elder brethren
who are gone hence ; say rather by entering into
the heart, the thoughts of God Himself, Who Alone
worketh all in us. And then, believe me, we shall
no longer find anything impossible ; we shall learn
how to accomplish that which God requires of man,
that for which He created him : the tilling and keeping
of His earthly paradise—" Posuit eum in Paradiso
voluptatis ut operaretur et custodiret illum " (Gen.
ii. 15.)—and the ordering of the world according to
equity and righteousness: "Deus qui constituisti
hominem, ut disponat orbem terrarum in justitia et
æquitate." (Wis. ix. 2.)

peuples demandent autre chose à leurs prêtres, et avec raison."
Mgr. Dupanloup.

CHAPTER VIII.

HENRI PERREYVE'S LAST DAYS.

HENRI PERREYVE returned rather suddenly to Paris from Pau, where he had been spending the winter, on April 9th, 1865. His family and friends, who had been deceived by the cheerful, hopeful tone of his letters during the last few months, were aghast at the state in which they really found him. Their alarm was too surely confirmed by the doctors; it was evident that the disease from which he had suffered for several years had made rapid progress.

Henri was not conscious of this; he looked upon his present condition as merely a passing ailment, and beguiled the weariness of illness with plans for the future. He talked of resuming his *cours* at the Sorbonne, in the coming half-year, and discussed the subject and scheme of the *discours* which he had to give before the Faculté de Théologie. All our attempts to alarm him and lead him not to be imprudent, either in going out, in over much conversation, or in excessive head work, were vain. Nevertheless, after a few weeks, he was forced to admit that his malady

P

did not yield to any efforts of medical skill; and he consented to go into the country. He was anxious to fulfil his Easter duties before going, these having been postponed in consequence of his being unable to pass the night without food. Now he hoped to be strong enough to say Mass himself on Sunday, April 30th, and not venturing to do so alone, he wrote the day before to ask me to assist on the occasion. But at the last moment his strength failed, and he could only make his confession. We spent a long time together, and it was settled that he should receive Holy Communion the next day. Accordingly, on Monday, May 1st, though hardly able to move even with the help of my arm, he came to receive his Easter Communion at my Mass, in the little chapel of the Pères de Sion, close to where he lived. He then went to Épinay, where after some faint glimmerings of amendment, it became past doubt that all treatment was useless, and that recovery was impossible. The sad tidings spread abroad among his friends, and their loving gratitude led to a union for prayer among a considerable number of those who loved him in various quarters of Paris, asking for the preservation of that dearly cherished young life. From this time Henri Perreyve realized his mistake as to the character of his illness; he saw that it was much more serious than he had supposed, and the thought of death became clear and vivid for the first time.[1] It did not cause him one moment's terror. He said to Charles Perraud (who, like myself, had been his intimate friend from childhood), "I have been thinking of death all this week, and I have accepted it without fear or regret; indeed, I have continually heard the *responsum mortis* within me. I am very grateful for the prayers offered for me, but I do not wish to live, and I cannot pray to do so. If I were to recover, I think and hope that I should do better, but perhaps even that is self-deceit. I am a poor invalid who thinks all would be easy if only he were once more strong."

One thing only troubled Henri as he contemplated death, and that he shared in common with all pure souls as they draw near to God's Perfect Holiness,—his conscious unworthiness and the memory of sin. At such times one had to encourage and reassure him by dwelling upon the thought of God's Mercy, and he would say in reply, "Yes indeed, I who so often preach God's Mercy to others should be able to trust myself to it."

He grieved much because he could not receive the Holy Communion as often as he would have wished, but he comforted himself by saying, "Even missionaries are sometimes obliged to go a long time without com-

---

[1] For the first time during this last phase of his illness; as we know, Henri Perreyve had looked death in the face more than once before this time.

municating ; and then too one does feel God very near one in privation."

Day by day Henri's strength wasted ; he could scarcely crawl out into the park surrounding the house in which he was staying, and he spent long hours alone in his room, giving himself up to an enjoyment of solitude which was altogether new to his eminently social nature, and saying, like Père de Ravignan, " I am never dull ; time does not seem long; I think and I pray." But while he was gently resolute in preserving this solitude from the interruptions even of those he loved best, it was readily sacrificed, as his whole life had been, to the duties of his sacred calling and the welfare of souls. Thus one day, a pupil from the École Militaire de Saint Cyr appeared at Épinay, and the door, which was so difficult of access to others, was instantly opened to him. A soul in need—a soul which probably had on some past occasion been touched by Henri's teaching at Sainte Barbe ;—ill as he was, Henri did not hesitate to give all the little strength he yet retained to this work of love, with his wonted affectionate earnestness. It was his last act of priestly ministration, and recalls to one's mind what Montalembert says of Père Lacordaire : " That noble being was like to God in that he loved our souls above all else—*Domine, qui amas animas nostras.*"

On Ascension Day (May 25th), after a Novena which had been offered for him, Henri was urgently and unexpectedly pressed to submit to a wholly fresh system of treatment. He hesitated considerably, and having finally consented, he observed to his friend, Père Charles Perraud, " I asked myself, as I often do, what Père Lacordaire would have done under similar circumstances, and I think he would have seen an indication of God's Providence in this." A few days later Henri returned to Paris, so as to be more immediately under his doctor's eye ; but this new effort of science and skill was as ineffectual as all else had been to check the malady, which was too deep-seated for cure, and which daily made rapid strides.

About a fortnight later (Wednesday, June 14th), a fainting fit came on suddenly, which alarmed Henri's sister exceedingly ; she sent for me, and begged me to go to Épinay and take counsel with their parents. Madame Perreyve was unable to leave Épinay owing to her husband's state of health, and she could only resign herself to wait, with the comfort of knowing that God's best blessing was around her dearly loved son. I returned to Paris to fulfil the office of telling my dear friend the exact state of things. It must always be a trying task to announce the immediate approach of death to any one ; but in this case it was

my solemn duty both as a priest and a friend. I
went into Henri's room at a time when he was feeling
so weak that the first thing he said was, "*Mon ami*,
only a few minutes to-day." A few minutes for such
a solemn task! But it had to be done, and I began
by dwelling upon his rapid worsening during the last
fortnight. He kept on answering me quietly, and
with an evident hopefulness which I could not share.
I prayed inwardly for help, and it came through the
patient himself. Something touched him suddenly,
and, without any connection with what he had been
previously saying, Henri exclaimed, "Oh! but one of
the things I feel most in dying is that I shall leave
you so alone in this life!" My tears fell too, but I
found courage to say, "Dear friend, now that for the
first time you have spoken so plainly of death, I must
tell you that we are very seriously anxious about you
to-day." He looked up at me, and said, with the
most perfect simplicity, "Really?" "Yes, we are all
very much alarmed, for you had a very serious fainting
fit this morning."

"You surprise me, I honestly confess; I knew that
I am very ill, but I did not think I was so near death.
Well, so much the better: but you must give me the
Holy Viaticum and Extreme Unction."

"I was thinking of that. Who would you like me
to ask to do it?"

"Why yourself, of course!" he answered; "only you must let Charles know, so that he may be present at so important an occasion."

"He is at hand," I said, "waiting for the result of our talk."

"Indeed!" Henri exclaimed, with some astonishment. "Then let it be directly;" and then he added, "Poor dear friend, how I thank you! What you have just done is not the least kindness you have shown me in your life! I know what it must have cost you. *Merci!*" After that he made Père Charles Perraud come in, and clung closely to him for some time.

I went to the parish church, Saint Sulpice, to fetch the Sacraments—that church which we had frequented together as children, where we received our First Communion, where, as lads, we had prayed and striven, where we had besought God to confirm our faith and keep us pure, where we had so often renewed our pledges of devoted service to Jesus Christ our Master, where we had both been ordained priests. That church had been the centre of our whole Christian life, and now one of the two was there to seek the last succours of the Church on behalf of his dying comrade!

On my return I found my dear friend up, and in an arm-chair; he had insisted on paying this token of respect to the Awful Presence he awaited. Henri

sent every one away, and made his confession to me,
speaking words of forgiveness and love, like his dear
Master on the Cross, and repeated the Magnificat
with me. I then summoned his sister and Charles
Perraud, who held open the office book in which
Henri wished to follow the prayers and ceremonies of
Extreme Unction, so as to make the responses himself. I began to administer the last Sacraments,
giving him no further preparation than the glorious
language in which the Church addresses her children
as they draw near to eternity. Before giving him the
Holy Viaticum, I called upon him to make his profession of faith, by repeating the Creed, as it is the
wont for priests to do. He said it with a firm voice
and the deepest recollection, and then he made a
sign that he wished to speak. He said : " I ask
forgiveness of my parents, whose absence I mourn
over most tenderly, for whatever I have done to dis-
please or grieve them. I ask forgiveness of my friends
for the faults they have seen me commit ; I thank
them all for their stedfast affection, and entreat them
to pray for me for long after my death. Don't let
them say, as is too often said, ' He is in heaven.' Let
them pray, and pray much for me, I entreat. And
I ask your forgiveness " (turning to his servant,
Théodore) " for any bad example I have given
you. You have seen me in close quarters, it is a

trying way of seeing a man ; I commend myself to your prayers."

Then he said the Te Deum, that hymn of thanksgiving for this life, before partaking of the Bread of Life Everlasting. All God's many blessings were lovingly remembered then, I am certain, by our friend : his Christian education, his parents' love, the intense devotion of his sister, who had been as a guardian angel to him, the friends of his childhood and youth, to whom he had given and from whom he had received the stay which hearts united in the love of Jesus Christ know how to find, the precious friendship of Père Lacordaire, the many loving hearts which had brightened his life, the growing success which had given promise that one day he was to be a powerful and useful servant of souls, of his country, of the Church. Yes, all God's graces and gifts were thankfully acknowledged, and the tone of loving faith with which he uttered the last words before receiving the blessed Sacrament, "*In te, Domine, speravi, non confundar in æternum,*" will never be forgotten by those who heard it.

. When he had received the Lord's Body, Henri's face kindled with heavenly brightness, and after he had made his thanksgiving, he said to me, "You cannot think what inward happiness has filled me, ever since you told me that I am about to die."

That evening I informed the Archbishop of Paris [1] of Henri's condition. He was greatly moved, saying that in Henri Perreyve he should lose a priest on whose usefulness in the diocese he had very specially counted; and promised to come and see him the first thing on the morrow. Hearing this, Henri insisted on being dressed in his most correct ecclesiastical habit to receive the Archbishop, and, in spite of his great weakness, rose from the bed on which he lay, as his venerable Diocesan entered, and knelt to receive his blessing. He wished to be alone with the Archbishop, who remained a long time with him, but later Henri spoke with tender gratitude of Mgr. Darboy's kindness.

During the following days he saw the R. Père Pététot, Superior of the Oratory, his first master in the priestly life, Père Gratry, whose zealous disciple he had been, the Bishop of Sura (Doyen de la Faculté de Théologie), M. de Montalembert, the Prince de Broglie, M. Augustin Cochin, Mgr. Buquet, the Abbé Lagarde, Vicaire Général, the Curé of Saint Sulpice, General Zamoiski, Count Plater, and others whose warm interest and sympathy had been unfailing. Henri wished to take leave also of some of his old friends; and to one former schoolfellow, M. Gellé, he wrote asking him to come and see him, adding play-

---

[1] Monseigneur Darboy, martyred in Paris, May 23rd, 1871.

fully, that M. Gellé would find him " between life and death." He also asked to see Dr. Charles Ozanam, whose skill and affection had saved his life repeatedly during the last fifteen years, and commended himself to his loving prayers. Dr. Ozanam, who saw that all the resources of science were powerless to save his friend, mentioned the miraculous cures which had been performed the last year at the shrine of S. Vincent de Paul (among others that of a niece of General Caminade's), and suggested that Henri should be taken thither. He listened without any eagerness, but with simple confidence, and begged me to obtain the necessary authority from the Superior General of the Lazarists. But death was a more speedy agent than even our affection, and Henri had left this world before the end of a Novena which the Bishop of Orléans began by celebrating at the altar of Saint Vincent de Paul on Monday, May 19th. Another old friend was also summoned by Henri — Père Adolphe Perraud of the Oratoire. "Dear friend," he said on his entrance, "I wanted to see you to say farewell, but we shall not cease to work together for God and the Church; shall we?"

"I ought," he also said, "to be very grievously troubled because of all my sins, but nevertheless I am in the most perfect peace. Before you go," Henri added, "give me your blessing." "Most certainly,"

Père Perraud answered, "if you too, will give me yours." And the two priest friends, ere they parted for ever in this life, each gave the other his blessing, each kissed the hand he loved with human love, and venerated as consecrated by the touch of Christ's Body and Blood.

Three days after receiving Extreme Unction, Saturday, June 17th, Henri became so unwontedly silent that I became uneasy as to his soul's condition. I feared lest the heartiness and energy of those earlier days were past, and lest the bitterness of the actual death hour were overwhelming him. It was true that during the last few weeks he had shown a strong inclination for silence, and had spent hours alone at his special request. I remembered too, how during the last month of his life, Père Lacordaire would scarcely see anybody, clinging stedfastly to a restful solitude. which he felt to be the greatest help towards a more entire union with God ; and I felt that the disciple might be influenced by the same heavenly longings as the master. Nevertheless, I dreaded his being tried by any inward struggles of anxiety or distress, and I questioned him. " No," he answered ; " God still gives me grace to abide in the same state of absolute resignation to His Will. I was rather fretted and troubled when death did not come quicker after what you told me ; and sometimes I have felt afraid lest I should grow impatient if this weariness and langour lasts very long, but on the whole I do resign myself absolutely to God."

Again he said, " Now more than ever I bless God for having taught me a simple religion, which goes straight to Jesus Christ, and is summed up in that one word of His Passion, FIAT. And then, too, when my heart grows dull, I think over some of those noble Platonic ideas concerning Eternal Beauty, and so I make philosophy help to bring my mind back to a religious train."

Sunday, June 18th, was the festival of Corpus Christi, a day he was wont to spend at Saint Sulpice ; I went to see him in the afternoon. He was in his arm-chair, but exceedingly weak, and almost immediately lay down upon his bed. As soon as he had done so, he asked me to read the 8th chapter of the Epistle to the Romans to him, a passage of Holy Scripture on which he had been wont to delight to meditate at the foot of the Cross in the Coliseum at Rome. Just before, without any further explanation as to what troubled him, he had indicated some inward trial by praying audibly before me, " *Domine, adauge nobis fidem.*" Doubtless it was with the object of soothing this trouble of his soul that Henri sought to hear anew Saint Paul's glorious words of immortal hope for those whose whole faith is in Jesus Christ.

I give the words as I read them, and whoever will read them thoughtfully from our point of view will perceive what deep feelings those solemn words were calculated to excite in two friends such as we were : one awaiting death, the other pointing his brother to eternity.

1. "Nihil ergo nunc damnationis est iis qui sunt in Christo Jesu, qui non secundum carnem ambulant. [1]

2. Lex enim spiritus vitæ in Christo Jesu liberavit me a lege peccati et mortis.

5. Qui enim secundum carnem sunt, quæ carnis sunt, sapiunt ; qui vero secundum spiritum sunt, quæ sunt spiritus, sentiunt.

6. Nam prudentia carnis, mors est : prudentia autem spiritus vita et pax.

7. Quoniam sapientia carnis inimica est Deo ; legi enim Dei non est subjecta : nec enim potest.

8. Qui autem in carne sunt, Deo placere non possunt.

9. Vos autem in carne non estis, sed in spiritu ; si tamen

---

[1] 1. "There is therefore now no condemnation to them which are in Christ Jesus, who walk not after the flesh, but after the Spirit.

2. For the law of the Spirit of life in Christ Jesus hath made me free from the law of sin and death.

5. For they that are after the flesh do mind the things of the flesh, but they that are after the Spirit the things of the Spirit.

6. For to be carnally minded is death, but to be spiritually minded is life and peace.

7. Because the carnal mind is enmity against God, for it is not subject to the law of God, neither indeed can be.

8. So they that are in the flesh cannot please God.

9. But ye are not in the flesh, but in the Spirit, if so be that

spiritus Dei habitat in vobis. Si quis autem spiritum Christi non habet, hic non est ejus.

10. Si autem Christus in vobis est ; corpus quidem mortuum est propter peccatum, spiritus vero vivit propter justificationem.

11. Quod si spiritus ejus qui suscitavit Jesum a mortuis, habitat in vobis, qui suscitavit Jesum Christum a mortuis, vivificabit et mortalia corpora vestra, propter inhabitantem spiritum ejus in vobis.

18. *Existimo enim, quod non sunt condignæ passiones hujus temporis ad futuram gloriam, quæ revelabitur in nobis.*

19. Nam exspectatio creaturæ revelationem filiorum Dei exspectat.

22. Scimus enim quod omnis creatura ingemiscit, et parturit usque adhuc.

23. Non solum autem illa, sed et nos ipsi primitias Spiritus habentes, *et ipsi intra nos gemimus, adoptionem filiorum Dei exspectantes, redemptionem corporis nostri.*

28. Scimus autem quoniam diligentibus Deum omnia co-

---

the Spirit of God dwell in you. Now if any man have not the Spirit of Christ, he is none of His.

10. And if Christ be in you, the body is dead because of sin ; but the Spirit is life because of righteousness.

11. But if the Spirit of Him that raised up Jesus from the dead dwell in you, He that raised up Christ from the dead shall also quicken your mortal bodies by His Spirit that dwelleth in you.

18. *For I reckon that the sufferings of this present time are not worthy to be compared with the glory which shall be revealed in us.*

19. For the earnest expectation of the creature waiteth for the manifestations of the sons of God.

22. For we know that the whole creation groaneth and travaileth in pain together until now.

23. And not only they, but ourselves also, which have the first fruits of the Spirit, *even we ourselves groan within ourselves, waiting for the adoption, to wit, the redemption of our body.*

28. And we know that all things work together for good

operantur in bonum, iis qui secundum propositum vocati sunt sancti.

30. *Quos autem prædestinavit, hos et vocavit ; et quos vocavit, hos et justificavit ; quos autem justificavit, illos et glorificavit.*

31. Quid ergo dicemus ad hæc? Si Deus pro nobis, quis contra nos?

32. Qui etiam proprio Filio suo non pepercit, sed pro nobis omnibus tradidit illum ; quomodo non etiam cum illo omnia nobis donavit?

33. Quis accusabit adversus electos Dei? Deus qui justificat.

34. Quis est qui condemnet? Christus Jesus, qui mortuus est, imo qui et resurrexit, qui est ad dexteram Dei, qui etiam interpellat pro nobis.

35. Quis ergo nos separabit a charitate Christi? tribulatio? an angustia? an fames? an nuditas? an periculum? an persecutio? an gladius?

---

to them that love God, to them who are the called according of His purpose.

30. *Moreover whom He did predestinate, them He also called ; and whom He called, them He also justified ; and whom He justified, them He also glorified.*

31. What shall we say then to these things? If God be for us, who can be against us?

32. He that spared not His own Son, but delivered Him up for us all, how shall He not with Him also freely give us all things?

33. Who shall lay anything to the charge of God's elect? It is God that justifieth.

34. Who is he that condemneth? It is Christ that died, yea rather that is risen again, Who is even at the Right Hand of God, Who also maketh intercession for us.

35. Who shall separate us from the love of Christ? Shall tribulation, or distress, or persecution, or famine, or nakedness, or peril, or sword?

36. (Sicut scriptum est : Quia propter te mortificamur tota die ; æstimati sumus sicut oves occisionis.)

37. Sed in his omnibus superamus propter eum qui dilexit nos.

38. Certus sum enim, *quia neque mors, neque vita,* neque Angeli, neque principatus, neque virtutes, neque instantia, neque futura, neque fortitudo,

39. Neque altitudo, neque profundum, *neque creatura alia poterit nos separare a charitate Dei, quæ est in* CHRISTO JESU DOMINO NOSTRO."

At the words, "Whom He did predestinate, them He also called ; and whom He called, them He also justified ;—and whom He justified, them He also glorified,"—I looked up at my friend to see what impression these words, which stirred my soul to its very depths, were making upon his soul. Our eyes met, tears filled those of both ; we pressed one another's hand silently, and I went on. But each word fed the strong emotion which well-nigh overpowered us. Jesus Christ was indeed with us, as with the disciples at Emmaus. He was speaking to

---

36. (As it is written, for Thy sake we are killed all the day long, we are accounted as sheep for the slaughter.)

37. But in all these things we are more than conquerors through Him that loved us.

38. For I am persuaded *that neither death, nor life,* nor angels, nor principalities, nor powers, nor things present, nor things to come,

39. Nor height, nor depth, *nor any other creature shall be able to separate us from the love of God, which is in* CHRIST JESUS OUR LORD."

us, and our hearts burned within us. I could scarcely
go on reading the sacred words ; Henri cried quietly.
But at the last words, " Neither death nor life . . .
shall be able to separate us from the love of God,"
our hitherto repressed feeling broke forth ; our tears
became sobs, and Henri, squeezing my hand, said,
" Oh, leave me alone with God ! *à demain !*"

I rose up in deep awe, to go, when he exclaimed,
" Or rather give me the Holy Communion."

In all haste I went to fetch the Blessed Sacrament,
gave it him, and without breaking the solemn silence
which filled our hearts by a single word, I left him
peacefully making his act of Thanksgiving, inwardly
entreating God to take my dear friend to Himself that
very night.

But that prayer was not granted ; he had yet somewhat more to suffer for Christ.

The days which followed were spent in waiting for
death. Henri said to Père Charles Perraud, " I see
now what a good thing it is to have had the habit of
thinking of death as a happy and wished-for thing."
And another time he said, " I never was so put out
at anything as not to be able to die all this time !"

His great emaciation was a constant cause of
suffering, and the fits of coughing which came on
from time to time were very terrible, but as hereto-
fore, Henri never complained : once he said to Père

Charles Perraud, " I set God's Will before me as a citadel on a high rock, to which I fly for refuge, and then I say, I know no other shelter ! " And another time he said : " What a blessing it is to be a Christian ! I never fully realized it before ; you may remember that all your life."[1]

About the middle of the week, the delusive rally which not uncommonly precedes death in such cases, rekindled those thoughts of life which Henri had so willingly laid aside : " It is a pity," he said to me : " I had grown accustomed to the thought of death : I accepted it and was happy in it, and now there will be a harder sacrifice to make, to accept a miserable weary life ! What a useless wretch I shall be for ever so long ! It must take two years at least to make up all the lost ground. Ah, I would rather have died ! There is one bright side to life though ; I will try to lead a better one, to be more thoroughly priestly, to do more good, and above all, to do it better. But after all, God's Will be done in life or in death ! "

But these deceptive appearances were short-lived ; the malady grew worse, and his strength failed faster than ever. On Sunday night, the Sister who nursed him warned me that she thought him much worse, and felt anxious as to the night. I therefore deter-

---

[1] " Tu pourras prêcher cela toute ta vie."

mined not to leave him any more. I went to him ;
he received me with a sadly sweet smile, saying, " I
am very weak, but better in some ways ; I felt my
nerves alive to-day, which I have not done for three
months. I hope I may have a good night." I em-
braced him, and gave him my blessing, not telling
him that I was going to stay in the adjoining room.
The night was restless and bad, and the next morning
he was so exhausted that the Sister begged me to tell
his family that he would scarcely live through the day.
She was right. It was Monday, June 26th; I went to
say Mass for him at the nearest church, feeling sure
that the end was near; on my return I went into
Henri's room. Probably I had not fully controlled
my expression, for he noticed it, and looking at me
fixedly, asked, " Is there anything fresh ? I wish to
know the truth." " Nothing particular," I answered,
" but I see a great change in you since last evening ;
I am very uneasy." " Indeed I feel much weaker,"
he said ; " probably it is natural that one should be
exhausted after a sleepless night, but I have a strange
sensation, a sort of numb dislocation of my very being.[1]

Well, I will try to rest a little. Adieu ! "

[1] Do not these words recall that striking passage in Gerontius'
Dream :—

" ''Tis death, O loving friends, your prayers ! 'tis he !
As though my very being had given way,

"Do so," I said, "but I shall not go away; I will stay either by your bed or in the next room."

"Why?" he asked; "am I really much worse?"

"I think you may be," I said—"at all events I shall not leave you; you may want me; you may wish to be confessed or communicated, and besides I promised the Sister to stay till she comes back."

"I understand," he said; "then it will be to-day. Very well, you must get me ready for the last great struggle; you must bring me the Holy Viaticum."

I confessed him for the last time, using the plenary indulgence for the dying, which was practically telling him how matters stood. Then he received the Holy Communion with the deepest devotion and peace, asking afterwards, as he always did, to be left awhile alone with God.

During the course of the morning he asked for Père Charles, and had some loving confidential talk with him; but life was sinking rapidly and visibly,

As though I was no more a substance now,
And could fall back on naught to be my stay,
(Help, loving Lord! Thou my sole Refuge, Thou,)
And turn no whither, but must needs decay
And drop from out this universal frame
Into that shapeless, scopeless, blank abyss,
That utter nothingness of which I came:
This is it that has come to pass in me;
O horror! this it is, my dearest, this;
So pray for me, my friends, who have not strength to pray."

though without any marked effort.   He suffered from
a general discomfort, which caused him occasionally
to groan and say, "What pain!" but quickly
followed by "God's Will be done."   When his doctor
came, Henri said, "It has come to that now that I
need only ask if you can give me any relief, for sometimes my suffering is so great that I am afraid of
growing impatient."

In the afternoon he pressed me earnestly, as he
had already several times pressed the Sister and Père
Charles, to tell him the fullest truth as to his condition.   I thought it only right to be quite open in
reply to what was asked with such trusting earnestness, and not to deprive that noble soul of the great
blessing of watching the approach of death, contemplating each step, which was all too slow for his
desires, and resigning himself into God's Hands with
all the fulness of willing love.   So I told him that we
could not count upon his living through the night,
perhaps not even through the day.   He thanked me
most affectionately for telling him, and then asked to
be left alone.   We kept watch at a little distance.
Before long Henri asked for his excellent father, who,
while sorely tried by his bodily infirmities, had in no
degree failed in the fullest mental life and vigour.   On
seeing him Henri said, "You must be brave; love is
strength, and God is more than all, dear father.   He

upholds one through the sharpest anguish. I feel
that now more than ever."

His father, mother, and sister knelt by his bed-side,
and he blessed them in the Name of Jesus Christ, Whose
priest he was. A little later he thanked the Sister who
had nursed him so tenderly. "A thousand thanks to
you, ma Sœur—let me have your Crucifix, not mine,
yours—which has been pressed to so many dying lips;"
and he kissed it lovingly saying, "Amen." He asked
to see the servants; thanked them for all they had done
for him, commended himself to their prayers, and gave
them his blessing. Dr. Gouraud came, and Henri
thanked him gratefully for his devoted friendship, and
his attempts, during these last days, to prolong his
life, adding quietly and kindly that it was useless
to give him any further trouble. His mother was
beside him, and he observed to her, "If I die to-
morrow, it will be the anniversary of my first Communion." "Dear child," she answered, weeping,
"how happy I was on that day, and you too!"
"Well," Henri replied, "we must be happy to-
morrow too." He made his sister stay by him while
he detailed certain alterations he wished to be made
in the family tomb, and with a clear firm voice told
her what was to be his epitaph: "Satiabor cum
apparuerit Gloria Tua." "When I awake up after
Thy Likeness, I shall be satisfied with It."

His whole soul was indeed poured forth in this utterance of faith, hope, and love.

From this time Henri was really in his last agony ; it was quiet and peaceful, but it was an agony—the last struggle of life resisting death.　His hands grew icy cold, his pulse scarcely perceptible ; the heavy oppression increased ; the body was fast perishing, but the soul retained all its faculties to the uttermost, and was stedfastly cleaving to God ; from time to time he put the Crucifix which he still held to his lips murmuring, "Lord, have mercy upon me ;" "Jesus, take me soon ;" "Jesus, come quickly:" and when his heaving breast could no longer yield breath for even such brief prayers, he still from time to time whispered gently the one word "Jesus."

Towards seven o'clock dear Henri made a sudden effort to raise himself in his bed.　His face was haggard and bathed in death sweat, his lips blanched, but his kindling eyes sparkled as he fixed them with the keenest expression of terror on some invisible but present enemy, and twice he cried out loudly, "I am afraid !　I am afraid !"　I hastened to his side saying, "No, no, you must not fear God, you must give yourself up wholly to His Mercy, and say 'In Thee, O Lord, have I trusted, let me never be confounded.'"　He looked up into my face, and said, "It s not of God I am afraid ! Oh no !—I am afraid, lest

I should be hindered dying!" I made him kiss his Crucifix, and he grew calm. Kneeling close beside him, and holding Père Lacordaire's cross, which he had had beside him all the day, I said slowly and distinctly, " My God, I love Thee with all my heart for time and for eternity."

" Oh yes ! with all my heart ! " he answered, and his dying lips clung to the likeness of our Dear Lord and Master Jesus Christ.

Those were his last words, his last act of faith and love.

The cold shadow of death fell upon that beautiful brow, his hitherto clear bright consciousness was veiled, and for a few minutes only the heaving breast told us that the soul had not yet fled. The two Fathers Charles and Adolphe Perraud said the last prayers for the dying—" Proficiscere, anima Christiana ; " " Go forth, O Christian soul." It was nearly eight in the evening. A last struggle set in, and I repeated over the soul which was yet held by its earthly chains, the sacramental words, " Ego te absolvo a peccatis tuis ; "—and then my voice rose amid the tears and sobs of loving friends and dear relations, crying out to the Throne of God, " De profundis clamor ad Te, Domine, quia apud Dominum miseri-cordia et copiosa apud eum Redemptio."

www.ingramcontent.com/pod-product-compliance
Lightning Source LLC
Chambersburg PA
CBHW031953060726
47497CB00016B/1979